BEYOND TIES THAT BIND

A Novel

MICHAEL MANOSCA

"Your children are not your children.
They are the sons and daughters of Life's longing
    for itself.
They come through you but not from you,
And though they are with you yet they belong not
    to you."

Kahlil Gibran, The Prophet (1923)

Contents

Part IV

RESOLUTION

Introduction to the
Second Edition

Many years ago, I was telling a story to friends over dinner at a little Thai place I frequented in Chicago. They insisted I write it down.

"I'm no author," I said.

But they told me that, contrary to my lack of belief in myself, I had plenty of stories from my travels and interactions with folk all over the world—and many would make great books. I appreciated their confidence, but I deflected, and we moved on to other topics.

I still don't see myself as an author in the traditional sense. This is not how I make my living. But I wondered: could I actually write a book? Isn't that cliché? Everyone is always "working on their novel," right? I live in California and worked for many years in the entertainment industry, so I've seen plenty of aspiring writers—what my grandmother would call "creative types"—come and go.

But me? Phew.

A few years back, bored with everything in my life, I thought of that conversation in Chicago and wondered: What would it take?

Plenty of work, that's for sure. And patience. And fortitude. And a willingness to actually do it.

So I set out to write a story that had been mulling around in my head for years. It was about me, really. I grew up wanting to be an artist. I thought I might be okay at it—won a few awards, did well in art school for a while. But I also met someone who changed my life. Someone who was so carefree and outgoing and spirited in ways I could never imagine myself to be. I wanted to pay tribute to him. And perhaps share a bit of my own journey along the way.

It was quite the fashion to share one's coming out story for a while there, but I didn't want to make this a "gay book," per se. I wanted it to be a story about finding yourself, about family—the one you're born into and the one you choose—and about learning to accept love when you're not sure you deserve it.

So I struggled. And I wrote. A lot. Too much, in fact.

My mind absorbs details and remembers everything. And I mean *everything*. I can recall the date and time the Christmas episode of The Mary Tyler Moore Show first aired on CBS in the '70s. The outfit I was wearing as a kid watching it. How I felt. How the house was decorated. Says a lot about me, doesn't it?

All of that went into my manuscript. And 650-odd pages later, I came up for air.

Then I began to edit.

Editing, by the way, is an art I have not perfected—and I wish I could. The story might be sound, but who cares if the author is droning on and on? It wasn't until much later, several novels in fact, that I turned to an actual editor for help. Bless her; I do not know how she gets through it all.

After a full year of writing and several rounds of self-editing, I put the book out there. More out of exhaustion than pride. I knew there were some good ideas in it. I felt a personal connection to the story. I was proud I'd actually written that much. But, as one reviewer put it—not so politely—there were just too many damn words. I didn't need to describe every detail of a Coca-Cola can my character was holding.

I pulled it from the market. Embarrassed, actually.

And it sat. For another year.

But something kept gnawing at me—a feeling that I should go back and give it a haircut. Let the face of the story shine through.

What lies ahead of you is that revision. Technically, a "revised" second edition. Truly, it's the version I didn't know how to write before. I trimmed nearly a third of the original manuscript—not to shorten it for the sake of brevity, but to give Alex and Jaime room to breathe. To let their personalities speak for themselves, rather than burying them under my endless descriptions and observations. They deserved that much.

I've since published multiple other novels and have four manuscripts in various stages of drafting. I've learned a thing or two, though I know I can still improve. I'm still learning.

For those few who read the first edition: bless you for coming around for more. For those who are new to the world of Alex and Jaime, I hope this version does them justice.

I know I remember walking in their shoes, all those years ago.

PART I

DEPARTURE

1

Leap

Alex was stalling, and he knew it.

The roller board had been open on his bed for two hours. In that time, he'd reorganized his colored pencils, straightened the prints above his desk—Degas, a Seurat postcard, things his brothers called "boring old stuff"—and spent twenty minutes flipping through the dog-eared copy of *ARTnews* that had first told him about Oakwood's fine arts program. Now he was cross-legged on the floor, not packing, while the August sun crept across the carpet toward his feet.

This room was the one place he'd ever made sense. Out there —at school, at family dinners, at the endless basketball games, watching his brother Jimmy play—he'd always been slightly off, like a radio station not quite tuned in. But here, surrounded by his own things, he could almost forget that.

"Alex!" His mother's voice rose through the floorboards. "Jason's here!"

He didn't move.

Footsteps on the stairs. A knock that was really just a warning before Jason pushed the door open. He was carrying something flat, wrapped in brown paper, which he set on Alex's desk without comment before surveying the room.

"Dude." Jason took in the empty luggage, the scattered clothes on the chair, the general evidence of paralysis. "You're supposed to leave in like two hours."

"I'm aware."

Jason stepped over a pile of sketchbooks and dropped onto the bed, making the roller board bounce. He was wearing his Che Guevara shirt—the one he thought made him look revolutionary but really just made him look like every other kid who'd discovered politics sophomore year.

"Your mom seems stressed," Jason said.

"She's been cleaning the same three rooms since Tuesday."

"And you've been... what? Staring at your walls?"

"Thinking."

"About art school?"

"It's not art school." Alex finally looked up. "It's a liberal arts college. With a fine arts program."

"Same difference."

"It's really not."

"You're going to take art classes and make art and hang out with art people. That's art school."

Alex didn't have the energy to argue. Jason wasn't entirely wrong, anyway. He just wasn't precisely right either—and the distinction mattered to Alex in ways he couldn't quite articulate.

His eyes drifted to the brown paper package on his desk. Jason caught the glance.

"That's for later. Don't open it until you stop somewhere on the road. There's a card."

"Since when do you make rules?"

"Since you decided to have a breakdown instead of packing." Jason stood and pulled Alex up with him. "Come on. What's clean?"

They packed without talking at first. Jason handed him shirts;

Alex folded them and placed them in the luggage. There was something almost intimate about it—going through someone's clothes, deciding what made the cut. Anyone else and it would've been awkward. But Jason had been in this room a thousand times, sprawled on the bed complaining about homework, flipping through Alex's art books pretending to be interested. He knew which drawers stuck and which shirts Alex actually wore versus the ones his mom bought him.

The watercolor from eighth grade went in last — a small painting of a Victorian farmhouse he'd done for a class assignment years ago. It had started as nothing, really. Just another project most kids rushed through to get a grade. But somewhere between the sketch and the final brushstroke, something shifted. He'd found himself caring. Staying after class to get the light right on the porch. Using the cheap watercolors from the plastic tray like they were oils, layering color until the house looked like somewhere you could actually live.

His teacher gave him an A and hung it on the cork board with the others. Everyone said it was nice. But Alex had felt something else entirely — a quiet certainty he couldn't explain to anyone, not even himself. Like he'd glimpsed something true about who he might become.

When he brought it home, he'd been careful with the push pin, preserving the single hole like it mattered. And over the years, no matter how many times he rearranged his room, that painting never moved. Same spot. Same pin. A small, private anchor.

Jason didn't ask why. He already knew.

"YOU'RE big man on campus now," Alex said, keeping his voice light. "Senior year. Top of the food chain."

Jason scoffed. "Right. You and Brad abandoning me to rule the school."

"We're not abandoning you."

"Who am I gonna talk to in drawing class?"

It landed harder than Jason probably meant it to. Alex's hands stilled on a folded shirt. He wanted to say he'd miss him too—miss their talks, the way Jason made that class the one thing he actually looked forward to. But that wasn't how they talked.

"You could always text Brad," he said instead.

Jason scoffed again. "Yeah, right. Like Duke's next basketball star is gonna reply." He shoved a pair of jeans toward Alex. "He was always your friend more than mine."

"Brad liked you."

"Mmhhmm."

"Besides," Alex tried, "you're gonna be the star now."

"Yeah." Jason almost smiled. "At least I don't have to compete with your ass in drawing anymore. Mrs. Scott always liked you best."

"Did not."

"Bullshit."

But Jason was smiling now. He knew it was true—knew Alex was better than him and always had been. He also knew Alex couldn't see it in himself. Never could. Jason wished he'd be around to keep reminding him, especially at college. Alex needed that.

From downstairs, the clatter of dishes. His mother finding things to do with her hands.

"Check-in's at four, right?" Jason asked.

"Three-thirty."

"So you need to be on the road by one. At the latest."

"I know."

"Then why are you moving like you've got all day?"

Alex didn't answer. He zipped the luggage, smoothed a wrinkle that didn't need smoothing.

Jason watched him for a moment. "It's gonna be fine, you know."

"I know."

"Liar." But Jason said it gently. "Look—the longer you drag this out, the worse it gets. Trust me. Just... go. Get in your crappy car, drive the two and a half hours, and start your life. Okay?"

"My car's not that crappy."

"Dude, Jimmy calls it the Tetanus Mobile."

"Jimmy's an idiot."

"Jimmy's not wrong."

They hauled the roller board downstairs together, Alex on one end, Jason on the other. His mother appeared from the kitchen, wiping her hands on a dish towel she'd been wringing for the past hour. His father stood by the front door, arms crossed, wearing the expression he always wore when something was happening that he didn't know how to talk about.

"You've got everything?" his mom asked. "Sheets? Towels? That power strip we bought?"

"It's all in the car already. Just this and my bag."

Scotty wandered in from the living room. "You're actually leaving?"

"That's generally what happens when you go to college."

"Huh." Scotty considered this. "Can I have your room?"

"No," their mother said, at the same time Alex said, "Absolutely not."

Jimmy appeared behind Scotty, smirking. "Sure the Tetanus Mobile's gonna make it that far?"

"It made it to Cedar Point last summer."

"Barely. I thought we were gonna die on 71."

"And yet here you are. Alive. Disappointing everyone."

Jimmy flipped him off behind their mother's back, grinning. Alex bit back a laugh.

His mother pulled him into a hug that lasted too long and not long enough. She smelled like dish soap and the lavender lotion she kept by the kitchen sink. "You call when you get there."

"I will."

"I mean it. The moment you arrive."

"I know, Mom."

His father's hug was briefer, firmer. A clap on the back that said everything he wouldn't put into words. "Drive safe. Check your mirrors."

"I will."

"And don't speed through those small towns. They'll ticket you just for having out-of-county plates."

"I know, Dad."

Outside, the heat pressed down, thick with the smell of cut grass and hot asphalt. Alex loaded the luggage into the back of his car—a Corolla with a dent in the passenger door and an air conditioner that only worked on the highest setting. He'd saved two summers for this car. Washed dishes at the diner on Route 42, mowed lawns for half the neighborhood. It wasn't pretty, but it was his.

Jason's package went on the passenger seat. Alex caught himself glancing at it as he closed the door.

Jason hung back while Alex's family clustered on the porch. When Alex turned, Jason was standing by the driver's door, hands shoved in his pockets.

"Don't forget," Jason said, nodding toward the package. "When you stop. Not while you're driving."

"I know. Rules."

Jason glanced at the porch, then pulled him into a quick hug anyway. "Senior year's gonna suck without you."

Alex climbed into the car. The vinyl seat was hot enough to burn through his jeans. He started the engine—it caught on the second try, which was better than average—and rolled down the window.

"Text me when you get there?" Jason asked.

"Yeah."

He backed out of the driveway, shifted into drive, and pulled onto Maple Street. In the rearview mirror, his family shrank—his mother still waving, his father's arms still crossed, Scotty already heading back inside.

Jason, still standing on the lawn, one hand raised.

Alex turned onto Route 42, the familiar stretch of asphalt that led to the highway heading east. The Corolla rattled over a pothole and Jason's package slid across the passenger seat; he caught it before it hit the floor, set it back, kept driving.

The town fell away behind him. Cornfields opened up on either side of the road, endless rows stretching toward a sky that seemed bigger out here than it ever did at home. He passed the county line, then the exit for the outlet mall where his mom dragged the family every August for back-to-school shopping, then the water tower with its faded high school mascot—a painted warrior that looked more tired than fierce these days. Every mile marker was a thing he knew, a thing he was leaving.

The package sat on the passenger seat the whole time. Brown paper catching the afternoon light. He kept glancing at it, then back at the road, then at it again.

About an hour in, he pulled off at a gas station—one of those old ones with only two pumps and a handwritten sign advertising night crawlers. The kind of place his dad would've called "a real operation" in that dry way of his. Alex filled the tank, bought a Coke from the machine outside, and got back in the car.

The air inside had gone stale and hot. He cracked the window, opened the Coke, let the first cold sip settle before he reached for Jason's package.

The sketchbook inside was nicer than anything Alex had ever owned—leather cover, thick cream-colored pages, the kind he'd lingered over at the art supply store downtown but never let himself buy. Too expensive. Real artists bought sketchbooks like this. He just drew.

The card was tucked inside the front cover. Jason's hand-writing slanted across the page, messy and familiar:

You've always seen things the rest of us miss. That's not weird. That's a gift. Go use it.

-J

Alex read it twice. Then once more, slower.

That's not weird. That's a gift.

He sat with it for a minute, the Coke sweating in his hand, the highway humming past beyond the gas station lot. He wanted to call Jason. Tell him thanks, tell him he didn't know how to believe it, tell him he already missed him more than he'd expected to.

But Jason would just make a joke and tell him to keep driving.

So he did.

He slipped the card into the front pocket of the sketchbook, set it on the passenger seat where he could see it, and pulled back onto the highway.

An hour and a half to go.

2

Arrival

Alex knew the campus. He'd been here two months ago with his dad—a quick tour after the acceptance letter came, Bill driving while Alex sat in the passenger seat pretending to read the welcome packet. They'd walked the quad with a group of other incoming freshmen, seen the dining hall, poked their heads into an empty lecture room. The guide had offered overnight stays in the dorms, a chance to "experience the Oakwood community firsthand," but Alex had declined. He just needed to know where things were. The basics. What paperwork to bring, where to check in, how to find his room.

His dad had understood. Alex was a pragmatist that way—if he had to learn to swim, he'd rather just jump in than stand at the edge working up the nerve.

But that had been with his dad. Today, he was alone.

The parking lot was a disaster.

Move-in day had turned the small lot behind Harrison Hall into a slow-motion collision of minivans and SUVs, parents double-parked with hazards blinking, freshmen hauling mini-fridges across the asphalt while their mothers shouted instructions. Alex had circled three times already. His hands were tight on the steering wheel, knuckles going white.

Fourth lap. Nothing.

A Subaru with Vermont plates cut in front of him to snag a spot that wasn't actually a spot—just a gap between two cars that the driver seemed to think was close enough. Alex slammed his brakes.

"Are you fucking kidding me?"

The words came out before he could stop them. This was the thing about driving—it turned him into someone else. Someone with a mouth on him that would've made his mother faint. He'd discovered it sophomore year in Driver's Ed, when some asshole in a pickup had cut him off at an intersection and Alex had found himself screaming "Go fuck yourself!" at a complete stranger while his driving instructor stared at him in shock. He'd apologized for ten minutes afterward, face burning, unable to explain where that had come from.

It kept coming from there, apparently. Every time he got behind the wheel.

Fifth lap. His jaw was clenched so tight it hurt. He was going to have to park on the street somewhere and haul his stuff half a mile in this heat and this whole fucking day was already—

Someone was waving at him.

A guy about his age, blondish curls, standing at the edge of the lot near an empty spot. Both arms up, waving like he was trying to flag down a rescue helicopter. When he caught Alex's eye, he stepped back and pointed at the spot, grinning.

Alex pulled in. Killed the engine. Let out a breath that felt like it had been trapped in his chest since he'd hugged his mother goodbye.

The guy appeared at his window. "Figured you could use that," he said. "I've been watching you circle. Thought you were going to stroke out."

Up close, he looked like he'd just stepped off a beach somewhere—tank top, Ray-Bans pushed up on his head, an ease in his posture that didn't match the chaos around them. His smile was wide and automatic, the kind of smile that probably worked on everyone.

"Thanks," Alex managed. His voice came out flat, but he meant it.

"I'm Jaime."

"Alex."

"You're in Harrison, right? I saw your parking pass." Jaime nodded toward the sticker on Alex's windshield. "Me too. Third floor."

"Second."

"Nice. Neighbors." Jaime was already moving toward the back of the car, reaching for the trunk. "Need help carrying stuff up?"

"No. Thanks."

Two words. Polite enough on the surface, but something in the delivery—the flatness, the finality—landed harder than Alex meant it to. He saw it happen: Jaime's smile faltering, his shoulders drawing in slightly, his whole body shifting backward like he'd touched something hot. The easy confidence from a moment ago just... collapsed.

"Oh. Okay. Sure." Jaime stepped back from the car, shoving his hands in his pockets. "No problem. I'll just—yeah. See you around, I guess."

He was already turning away when Alex heard himself. Heard the cold dismissal in his own voice, saw the way he'd just swatted down someone who'd gone out of his way to help him, and felt something twist in his gut.

"Wait."

Jaime paused, half-turned.

"I'm sorry." Alex exhaled. "That was... I didn't mean it like that. It's been a long day. I'm tired and I'm—" He stopped. What was he supposed to say? That he turned into a different person when he was overwhelmed? That he had walls that went up automatically, even when he didn't want them to? "I'm sorry. That was shitty of me."

Jaime studied him for a moment. The performer's mask was gone now, replaced by something more cautious, more real. Then, slowly, he nodded.

"It's okay. Move-in day is brutal."

"Still. You saved me a parking spot. And I just..." Alex gestured vaguely, unable to finish the sentence.

"Bit my head off?"

"Yeah."

A pause. Then the corner of Jaime's mouth twitched—not the full-wattage smile from before, but something smaller, more genuine. "Apology accepted. For what it's worth, I've seen worse. You should've heard my mom when the moving company lost her grandmother's china."

Alex almost smiled. "That bad?"

"Three languages. Two of which I didn't know she spoke."

Alex popped the trunk. His life was packed in there—roller board, duffel bag, two boxes, the art supplies he couldn't leave behind. Not much, but enough. His things. The only familiar anchors he had now that his family, his room, Jason—all of it— was two and a half hours away.

"You can help carry some of it up," he said. "If you want."

Jaime grabbed one of the boxes before Alex could change his mind.

They walked toward Harrison Hall, Jaime filling the silence with easy chatter—nothing important, just observations about the campus, the chaos of move-in day, the humidity. Alex half-listened, still raw from the exchange at the car. But he noticed things. The way Jaime talked with his hands. The slight accent that placed him somewhere northeast, probably New York. The way his cheerfulness had come back, but different now—less automatic, more careful.

At his room—a single on the second floor, small but private—Alex unlocked the door and stepped inside. Jaime set the box down just inside the threshold and leaned against the doorframe, not entering.

"Thanks," Alex said again.

"No problem." Jaime glanced around the room—bare mattress, empty desk, cinder block walls. "You good? Need anything else?"

"I'm good. Thanks."

"Cool. I'm in 312 if you need anything." He gave a small wave and headed for the stairs.

After Jaime left, Alex stood in the middle of his room and breathed.

He spent the next two hours making it his. Sheets on the bed. Clothes in the closet. Art supplies arranged on the desk—pencils in the cup, sketchbooks stacked, the leather one from Jason placed where he could see it. The small watercolor went up on the wall above his desk — the one piece of color against the cinder block gray.

By the time he finished, the room looked less like a cell and more like somewhere he might actually be able to breathe. His things surrounded him—not his family, not Jason, but the next best thing. Anchors. Proof that he was still himself, even here.

Alex sat on the bed and let the silence settle. Back home, there was always something—his brothers fighting, his mom in the kitchen, the neighbor's dog, the hum of the town existing around him. Here, it was just quiet. The occasional door slamming down the hall. Footsteps. Then nothing.

He wasn't sure if he liked it or not.

A KNOCK on his door around six.

Alex opened it to find Jaime in the hallway—same tank top,

same shorts as before. He was leaning against the opposite wall, not the doorframe, keeping a respectful distance.

"Hey." Jaime gave a small wave. "Just wanted to check if you got settled in okay. I'm not—I mean, I don't want to bother you. I know you've got stuff to do."

There was something different about him now. The easy confidence from the parking lot was muted, more careful. Like Alex's earlier coldness had stuck with him, made him second-guess whether he was welcome.

"I'm good," Alex said. "Got everything put away."

"Cool. That's good." Jaime nodded, glanced down the hallway, then back. He made no move to come closer. "Your room looks nice. From what I can see."

An awkward pause. Jaime was clearly waiting for something —a dismissal or an invitation, unwilling to assume either.

"You can come in," Alex said. "If you want."

Jaime's eyebrows lifted slightly, like he hadn't expected that. He pushed off the wall and stepped to the threshold, but stopped there, one hand on the doorframe, still not quite entering.

"Yeah?" he asked. Making sure.

"Yeah."

Jaime stepped inside, looking around at what Alex had done with the space. The watercolor on the wall, the art supplies arranged on the desk, the sketchbooks stacked neatly. "Damn. You actually made it look like a room. Mine still looks like a..." He trailed off, something flickering across his face.

"Like a what?"

"Nothing. It's fine." Jaime waved it away, but Alex caught the edge of something underneath—frustration, maybe, or embarrassment. "I mean, there's not much I can do with it right now anyway."

Alex frowned. "What do you mean?"

"My stuff." Jaime shrugged, aiming for casual but not quite landing it. "The airline. They lost it this morning—both bags. Said it'd be here by tonight, but..." He gestured at himself, at the same clothes he'd been wearing all day. "Still waiting."

Alex stared at him. "Wait. You've been here all day with nothing?"

"Pretty much. I've got my phone, my wallet, the clothes I'm wearing. That's it." Jaime laughed, but it sounded hollow. "They said it's somewhere between New York and here. Very reassuring."

"So when you were helping me carry my stuff up—"

"I didn't have anything to carry myself. Yeah." Jaime shrugged again. "It's fine. It's not a big deal."

Alex had spent the last few hours building a cocoon against the strangeness of this place. Jaime had spent them arriving somewhere completely new with nothing—not even a change of clothes. Just a bare room and a wait that might never end.

"That's awful," Alex said quietly.

"It's fine. Really. I'm used to—" Jaime stopped himself. "It'll get here eventually."

"Have you eaten anything today?"

"What?"

"Food. Have you eaten?"

Jaime hesitated. "I grabbed a granola bar from a vending machine earlier. I wasn't sure where the dining hall was, and I didn't want to bother anyone to ask, so—"

"Come on." Alex grabbed his room key from the desk. "We're getting dinner."

Jaime blinked. "You don't have to—"

"You've been wandering around all day with no stuff and no food. We're getting dinner." Alex was already at the door. "You coming?"

Something shifted in Jaime's face—the performer falling away, replaced by something more real. Surprise, maybe. Or gratitude. Or just the relief of someone finally seeing through the "I'm fine" to the "I'm actually not fine at all."

"Yeah," Jaime said softly. "Okay. Yeah."

THE DINING HALL was loud and crowded and smelled like industrial pasta. They found a table near the windows and ate in something that wasn't quite comfortable silence—but wasn't uncomfortable either. Alex picked at his food, still too keyed up to be hungry. Jaime demolished a plate of chicken and rice like he hadn't eaten in days.

"So," Jaime said between bites, "why Oakwood?"

Alex shrugged. "Good fine arts program. Small. Far enough from home to feel like something different."

"But not too far."

"Right." Alex took a bite, then asked, "What about you? Did you visit before you decided?"

"Nope."

"Your parents didn't want to see it first?"

Jaime's fork paused for just a fraction of a second. "They offered. I said I didn't need to." He shrugged, the casual mask back in place. "Saw it online. Looked nice. Quiet."

Alex frowned slightly. "So today was your first day here? Ever?"

"Yep."

There was something underneath that—Alex could feel it. The way Jaime's answers got shorter, the way his eyes didn't quite meet Alex's. Not hiding something bad, exactly. More like... not ready to explain something he didn't fully understand himself.

Alex let it go. He understood about that, too.

"You said fine arts," Jaime said, steering them somewhere safer. "What's your thing? Painting? Sculpture? Underwater basket weaving?"

"Drawing, mostly. Some painting."

"That's cool. I can't draw a straight line." Jaime grinned. "Seriously, I tried once. It looked like a drunk snake."

"Drunk snakes are underrated."

Jaime laughed—a real one, not the polished performance Alex had heard earlier. "See, that's what I said. My art teacher disagreed."

They talked for another hour. Nothing important—hometowns, siblings (Alex's brothers, Jaime's only-child status), high school (Alex's quiet Ohio existence, Jaime's vague references to "the city" that Alex understood to mean New York). Jaime was easy to talk to, or at least easy to listen to. He filled silence naturally, but Alex noticed he also knew when to stop, when to let a pause breathe.

He also noticed the way Jaime deflected certain questions. Where exactly in New York? "Manhattan, Upper West Side." Why Oakwood specifically? "Wanted a change of pace." What did his parents do? "My dad was a dancer. Mom does... a lot of things." Each answer came with that same practiced smile, followed by a quick pivot to a new topic.

There was something underneath. Alex could feel it—the same way he could always feel the shape of something before he drew it, the negative space around an object, the weight of what wasn't being shown.

He didn't push. He understood about not wanting to show everything.

THEY WALKED BACK to Harrison as the sun dropped below the trees. The August heat had finally broken into something bearable, and the campus was quieter now, most families gone, the chaos of move-in day settling into something calmer.

At Alex's door, they stopped.

"Thanks," Jaime said. "For dinner. You didn't have to do that."

"You spent all day waiting for a phone call that never came. Least I could do."

"Still." Jaime looked at him—really looked, like he was trying to figure something out. "You're not what I expected."

"What did you expect?"

"I don't know. Someone more..." He waved his hand vaguely. "I don't know. You surprised me."

Alex didn't know what to say to that. He wasn't used to surprising anyone.

"Anyway." Jaime smiled, softer now. "I'll see you around, Alex."

He reached out and pulled Alex into a hug.

It happened fast—Jaime's arms around him, warm and unhesitant, the kind of full-body embrace that Alex's family never did. His father's hugs were brief and firm, a clap on the back. His mother's were soft but restrained, always ending with a pat. Jason's were rare, reserved for moments of real emotion, and even then, quick.

This was different. This lasted.

Alex stood rigid for a second, unsure what to do with his arms, with his body, with the sudden invasion of his space by someone he'd known for less than twelve hours. His heart hammered against his ribs.

Then, slowly, he let himself lean in. Just a little.

Jaime pulled back, still smiling, apparently unaware that he'd just done something seismic. "Welcome to Oakwood," he said. Then he turned and headed for the stairs, throwing a wave over his shoulder.

Alex stood in his doorway, watching until Jaime disappeared around the corner.

His hands were shaking. He noticed that as he fumbled with his room key. Shaking. From a hug.

He closed the door behind him and leaned against it, staring at the watercolor on the opposite wall—the one familiar thing looking back at him in a room that suddenly felt different than it had an hour ago.

What the hell just happened?

3

The Circle

The alarm clock went off, but Alex had already been awake.

He lay there listening to the unfamiliar sounds of dorm life—doors slamming down the hall, someone's shower running, laughter echoing from the stairwell. Different from home, where the noises had shape and meaning. Jimmy's music through the wall. Scotty padding to the bathroom at 2 AM. Here, everything was anonymous. Strangers living their lives on the other side of thin walls.

He got up, showered, pulled on jeans and a t-shirt. Coffee from the dining hall, black and bitter. By 8:30, he was crossing the quad toward Lincoln Hall, schedule folded in his back pocket.

"Hey—you heading to Lincoln?"

Alex turned. Jaime was jogging to catch up, backpack bouncing, looking more awake than anyone had a right to at this hour.

"Yeah."

"Me too. Western Lit, 8:45." Jaime fell into step beside him. "You?"

Alex almost groaned. "Same."

"Wait, seriously?" Jaime's face lit up. "That's great. At least we'll know someone."

They passed the bronze statue of Lincoln at the building's entrance. A group of upperclassmen were clustered nearby, one of them reaching out to touch the statue's left shoe—worn golden from years of contact.

"Wonder what that's about," Jaime said.

"No idea."

Inside, they climbed to the second floor and found LH207. The lecture hall was larger than any classroom Alex had seen— tiered seating curving around a central podium, long tables instead of desks. Already half-full.

Scanning for a seat in the back corner, somewhere against the wall where he could watch without being watched, he saw the back rows were already claimed.

"There's two," Jaime said, pointing toward the middle section. "Come sit with me?"

It wasn't where Alex would have chosen. But Jaime was already moving, and Alex found it easier to follow than to explain why he'd rather sit alone.

They slid into seats along one of the curved tables. Sitting his notebook down, he was acutely aware of how exposed he felt— students on all sides, no wall at his back.

A tap on his shoulder.

Alex turned to find a girl with an explosion of red curly hair grinning at him from the seat to his left. Freckled face, bright eyes, an energy that seemed to vibrate off her in waves.

"Hi! I'm Emma." She stuck out her hand. "Biochem major. Well, probably. I might switch to biomedical engineering, but that's a lot of syllables, you know? Anyway—first day! Isn't this wild?"

He shook her hand. "Alex."

"Alex! Great name. Very classic." She leaned past him to wave at Jaime. "Hi! I'm Emma!"

"Jaime." He was grinning, clearly delighted. "I like your energy."

"Thanks! I have a lot of it. My mom says it's a condition, but I prefer to think of it as a superpower." She turned back to Alex, studying him for a moment. "You're an artist, aren't you? You have that look."

"What look?"

"Like you're seeing things the rest of us miss." She said it matter-of-factly, like she was commenting on the weather. Before Alex could respond, she'd already pivoted. "So what's everyone doing tonight? There's a game night thing at the student center. New student welcome. Board games, free food. I'm going. You should come." This was directed at Jaime. "Both of you, obviously, but especially you. You seem fun."

"I'm in," Jaime said.

"Perfect! Seven o'clock. I'll find you if you're not there." She turned to the front as the professor appeared at the podium, apparently satisfied that she'd accomplished her mission.

Alex exchanged a glance with Jaime, who just shrugged, still smiling.

The professor—tall, wire-rimmed glasses, the resigned air of someone who'd given this speech many times—cleared his throat.

"Good morning. For most of you, this will be the first class of your undergraduate career. As such, you may refer to me as Professor Lyden, and once we get to know each other over the semester, you may then refer to me as..." He paused. "Professor Lyden."

A few students laughed. Emma elbowed Alex in the ribs, beaming like the joke was the funniest thing she'd ever heard.

The next forty minutes passed in a blur of syllabus review and textbook requirements. Alex took notes, half-listened, occasionally glanced at Jaime beside him—who was actually paying attention, pen moving across his notebook in surprisingly neat handwriting.

When class ended, Emma was already on her feet, somehow packed up before the professor finished speaking.

"Seven o'clock!" she called to Jaime, pointing at him as she backed toward the door. "Don't forget!" Then she was gone, swallowed by the crowd.

"She's something," Alex said.

"She's great." Jaime shouldered his backpack. "When's your next class?"

"Not until two. You?"

"Rhetoric at 10:15. Just upstairs." Jaime paused. "You going to that game night thing?"

"Probably not."

Jaime nodded, unsurprised. "Yeah, I figured. Well—see you later?"

"Yeah."

They parted ways at the stairs—Jaime heading up, Alex heading out into the bright morning sun.

THE KNOCK CAME AROUND SIX.

Alex had survived two more classes after Western Lit—an intro art history lecture that ran long and a figure drawing session that left his hand cramped—then retreated to his room. He'd spent the last two hours starting his homework, trying to get ahead before the workload buried him. He'd almost forgotten about the game night entirely.

He opened the door to find Jaime in the hallway, hands in his pockets.

"Hey. I know you said you weren't going, but I'm heading to that game night thing. Thought I'd ask again." He shrugged. "No pressure."

"I don't think so. I've got homework."

"Yeah, okay. That's cool." Jaime nodded, already stepping back. "I'll see you later, then."

But Alex saw it—the slight fall in Jaime's expression before he caught himself. Just a flicker, quickly masked. Most people wouldn't have noticed.

Alex wasn't most people.

Jaime was already turning away, and Alex stood there in the doorway, watching him go. He didn't want to go to game night. He wanted to stay here, in his room, with his homework and his silence and the comfortable walls he'd been building since he arrived. That was what made sense. That was who he was.

But Jaime had come back. Had knocked on his door again, even after Alex had made it clear he wasn't interested. No pressure, he'd said—and meant it. He hadn't pushed, hadn't guilt-tripped, hadn't made it weird. Just asked, accepted the no, and left.

Why did he keep showing up?

Alex didn't understand Jaime yet. Didn't know what to make of someone who kept reaching out to a person who clearly wanted to be left alone. But he understood this much: Jaime wanted to be his friend. For whatever reason, he'd decided Alex was worth the effort.

And Alex had just shut the door in his face. Again.

"Wait."

The word came out before he could stop it. Jaime paused at the top of the stairs, looked back.

"I'll come."

He felt uncomfortable the moment he said it. This wasn't him. He didn't do things like this—didn't change his mind, didn't let people pull him out of his comfort zone. But Jaime's face was already shifting—surprise, then a grin that spread slow and wide.

"Yeah?"

"But if it's terrible, I'm leaving."

"Deal."

. . .

THE STUDENT CENTER WAS CHAOS.

Tables everywhere, students clustered around board games, the clatter of dice and bursts of laughter. A guy in the corner was playing acoustic guitar, badly. The noise hit Alex like a wall, and for a moment he wanted to turn around and walk right back out.

But Emma had already spotted them.

"Jaime! Alex! Over here!" She was waving from a table near the windows, red hair impossible to miss. "I saved you seats!"

They made their way over. Two others were already at the table—a tall guy in a button-down shirt, sleeves rolled precisely to the elbow, and a dark-haired girl arranging game pieces with the focus of a surgeon.

"This is Carlos," Emma said, gesturing to the guy. "Sophomore. Political science. He's going to be president someday, or at least that's what he tells everyone."

"Vice president," Carlos corrected, standing to shake their hands. His grip was firm, formal. "Presidents get assassinated. Vice presidents get forgotten. Much safer." He smiled to show he was joking—mostly.

"And this is Maya."

The dark-haired girl glanced up from the game board. "Hi." Then back to her pieces.

"Maya's a physics major," Emma continued. "She's terrifying and also my favorite person here. Don't let her fool you—she's secretly nice."

"I'm not secretly anything," Maya said, still arranging pieces. "I'm exactly what I appear to be."

"See? Terrifying. I love her."

They settled into seats—Alex next to Jaime, across from Maya, with Emma and Carlos filling out the table. The game was Settlers of Catan, which Alex had played once years ago with Jason and Brad and remembered almost nothing about.

"Do you know the rules?" Maya asked, looking directly at Alex.

"Vaguely."

"Vaguely isn't good enough. Pay attention." And she launched into an explanation that was somehow both thorough and efficient, covering everything Alex needed to know in about two minutes.

The game started. Maya played like she was conducting a military campaign—precise, strategic, three moves ahead at all times. Carlos was more subtle, building steadily, never revealing his intentions. Emma played like she lived—chaotic, enthusiastic, making deals with everyone and somehow coming out ahead despite apparently having no plan at all.

Jaime was harder to read. He joked around, complimented good moves, seemed more interested in the social dynamics than the game itself. But Alex noticed him quietly accumulating resources, building roads in directions no one was watching. There was more going on beneath that friendly exterior than he let people see.

"Your turn," Maya said, snapping Alex back to the present.

He looked at the board, made a decision, placed a settlement.

Maya studied his move for a moment. Then, almost imperceptibly, she nodded.

From her, that was practically a standing ovation.

The game went another hour. Maya won—"obviously," Emma muttered—but it was closer than anyone expected. Alex came in third, which earned him an approving look from Maya and a dramatic slow clap from Emma.

Afterward, they sat around talking. Nothing important—classes, hometowns, complaints about the dining hall. Carlos told a story about his first week as a freshman that made everyone laugh. Emma described her high school chemistry teacher in terms that probably constituted slander. Maya offered exactly three comments, all of them dry and perfectly timed.

Alex mostly listened. But he laughed at the right moments, and he asked Carlos about his political science classes, and when

Maya made a quiet observation about the statistical improbability of Emma's dice rolls, he found himself smiling.

These weren't his friends. Not yet. He'd known them for two hours. But they could be, maybe. There was potential here—something he hadn't expected to find so quickly.

Around nine, people started leaving. Carlos had early reading to finish. Maya had "work"—she didn't specify what kind, and no one asked. Emma extracted promises from everyone to do this again, then bounced off to introduce herself to a table of students she didn't know yet.

Alex and Jaime walked back to Harrison Hall together, the campus quiet around them.

"So," Jaime said. "Terrible?"

"What?"

"You said if it was terrible, you'd leave. You didn't leave."

Alex considered this. "It wasn't terrible."

"High praise." Jaime was smiling—that smile that seemed to come so naturally to him, so foreign to Alex's own experience. "Emma's a lot, but she's good people. Carlos too. Maya scares me a little, but I think that's the point."

"She's not so bad. She just doesn't waste words."

"Unlike some of us." Jaime glanced at him. "Thanks for coming. I know you didn't want to."

"How do you know I didn't want to?"

"Because you said no three times before you said yes. And you looked like you were going to bolt for the first twenty minutes."

Alex didn't have a response to that. Jaime was right. He had wanted to stay in his room, alone, safe. But he'd gone anyway, because Jaime had asked—not demanded, not pressured, just asked—and something about that had made it possible to say yes.

He wasn't sure what to do with that information.

They reached Harrison Hall. Inside, up the stairs, Alex stopping at the second floor landing while Jaime continued up toward the third.

"See you tomorrow?" Jaime asked from above.

"Yeah. Tomorrow."

Jaime disappeared up the stairs. Alex stood there a moment longer, then went to his room and closed the door behind him.

He sat on his bed, thinking.

He'd met people tonight. People who might become friends, given time. People who'd included him without making a big deal of it, who'd let him be quiet when he needed to be quiet and pulled him in when he started to drift too far toward the edges.

It shouldn't have been remarkable. But for Alex, it was.

He thought about Jaime showing up at his door, hands in pockets, no pressure. The slight disappointment in his face when Alex had started to say no. The way he'd accepted Alex's reluctance without pushing, and somehow that acceptance had made it easier to change his mind.

Why did Jaime care? Alex wasn't exactly the kind of person who drew people in. He was quiet, guarded, more comfortable alone than in crowds. Most people took one look at him and decided he wasn't worth the effort.

Jaime kept making the effort anyway.

Alex didn't know what to make of that. Didn't know what it meant, or what he was supposed to do with it.

If anything.

4

Mirrors

Emma needed a dress.

Not just any dress—a dress for her interview at the campus tutoring center, which she'd somehow convinced herself required looking "professional but approachable, like a friendly scientist." Alex wasn't entirely sure what that meant, but Emma had been talking about it for three days straight, and Jaime had finally declared that the only solution was a shopping trip.

"Eastwick Village," Jaime announced at lunch on Friday. "There's a Nordstrom. Emma can find something perfect."

"You should come too," Emma said, turning to Alex with that look she got when she'd already decided something and was just waiting for everyone else to catch up.

Alex's instinct was to decline. A shopping trip with Emma and Jaime sounded exhausting—all that energy, all that socializing, all those decisions about things he didn't care about. He could already feel himself wanting to retreat to his room.

But Jaime was looking at him with that quiet expectation, and Emma was practically bouncing in her seat, and somewhere in the past few weeks, saying no to these two had gotten harder.

"Fine," he said. "But I'm not trying anything on."

"We'll see about that," Jaime said, and something in his smile suggested Alex had already lost that battle.

The shuttle left from the transportation center at five. Alex had offered to drive—his car was sitting in the lot, after all—but Jaime had declined with a diplomacy that suggested he remembered the parking lot incident all too well.

"The shuttle's easier," he'd said. "No stress."

What he meant was: I've seen you behind the wheel.

Fair enough.

Watching Emma and Jaime on the shuttle, Alex found himself thinking about how well they fit together. They had the same energy—bright and outgoing, filling silence effortlessly, making friends with strangers like it was the most natural thing in the world. Two peas in a pod, his mother would say.

He wondered, not for the first time, if there was something between them. They'd clicked from the first moment in Western Lit, finishing each other's sentences, sharing jokes Alex didn't always follow. It would make sense. Emma was pretty in her own chaotic way, and Jaime was... well, Jaime was Jaime. They made sense together in a way that Alex, quiet and awkward and perpetually on the outside, never quite did with anyone.

The thought settled somewhere uncomfortable in his chest. He wasn't sure why.

EASTWICK VILLAGE WAS NOT A MALL.

Jaime made this very clear as they stepped off the shuttle into what looked, to Alex, exactly like a mall.

"It's an outdoor shopping experience," Jaime explained. "Very different vibe."

"There's a Gap and a Starbucks."

"Yes, but they're arranged around a central courtyard with fountains. Completely different."

Alex decided not to argue.

Nordstrom anchored one end of the "experience," its gleaming entrance promising a world Alex had never really inhabited. His shopping typically consisted of whatever was on sale at the outlet stores his mom dragged the family to every August—functional clothes in neutral colors that wouldn't draw attention.

Jaime, apparently, had opinions about this.

"Rule one," he said as they entered the women's department. "Never shop alone. You need someone else's eyes. We all have blind spots about ourselves."

"I shop alone all the time," Alex said.

"And how's that working out for you?"

The words landed sharper than Jaime probably intended. Alex looked down at his jeans and plain t-shirt—the same kind of thing he'd been wearing since middle school.

Jaime caught himself. His expression shifted, something like regret flickering across his face.

"Hey—I'm sorry." He reached out and touched Alex's arm, just briefly. "That came out wrong. My New York is showing. I didn't mean—"

"What's wrong with the way I look?"

Alex kept his face neutral, watching Jaime squirm.

"Nothing! Nothing's wrong. You look fine. Good, actually. I just meant—" Jaime was actually flustered now, hands moving as he tried to backtrack. "I meant that everyone can benefit from a second opinion, not that you specifically—"

Alex let the corner of his mouth twitch upward.

Jaime stopped mid-sentence. Stared at him. Then broke into a grin.

"You're messing with me."

"Little bit."

"You're an asshole."

"Little bit."

Jaime laughed—surprised, delighted—and something passed between them. A recognition. Alex wasn't just the quiet guy who tagged along. There was more underneath, if you knew where to look.

Emma appeared from behind a rack of dresses, arms already full. "Are you two done flirting? I need opinions."

Neither of them corrected her.

WATCHING JAIME in his element was fascinating.

He moved through the racks with purpose, pulling dresses, holding them up to Emma, discarding some immediately and setting others aside. He knew about cuts and colors and something called "undertones" that Alex had never heard of. He spoke to the sales associate like they were colleagues, using vocabulary Alex couldn't follow.

What kind of guy knew all this?

Alex's father certainly didn't. Bill Robertson bought the same brand of khakis he'd worn for twenty years and considered a "nice shirt" to be one without stains. Jason was the same—clothes were functional, not interesting. Even Brad, with all his money, just wore whatever was popular without thinking about it.

But Jaime talked about fashion like Alex talked about art. Like it mattered. Like it meant something.

Alex found himself watching more closely. The way Jaime's hands moved when he was explaining something. The way his face lit up when he found the right piece. The way he seemed so comfortable in this world that felt completely foreign to Alex.

There was something about it that caught his attention. He wasn't sure what.

"Okay," Emma announced, emerging from the dressing room in a navy blue dress. "What do we think?"

She did a small turn in front of the tri-fold mirror. The dress was nice—Alex could see that much. It made her look older, more professional. But something about the way she was standing felt off.

"I love it!" Emma said to her reflection.

"I wasn't asking you." Jaime turned to Alex. "What do you think?"

"Me?"

"You're the artist." Jaime's voice had shifted—less playful now, more serious. "If you were going to draw her right now, how would you pose her?"

Alex stared at him. It was such a strange question.

But Jaime was waiting. And Emma had turned from the mirror, curious now, watching him.

"Can I...?" Alex gestured vaguely.

"Go for it," Emma said.

Alex stepped closer to the mirror, studying Emma's reflection from all three angles. The dress was right—the color worked, the fit was good. But the way she was holding herself was stiff, uncertain. She looked like someone wearing a costume, not someone inhabiting her own skin.

He closed his eyes.

It was easier this way—blocking out the fluorescent lights, the sounds of the store, the awareness that people were watching him. In the darkness behind his eyelids, he could see what he wanted: a Degas painting he'd studied for hours as a kid, a ballerina caught in a moment of stillness before a mirror. The way the light fell across her shoulders. The elegant line from her ankle through her hip. The quiet confidence in her posture.

He let the image settle over Emma like a transparency, aligning the real with the imagined.

Then he opened his eyes and began.

His hands moved without conscious thought—lifting Emma's right wrist, adjusting the angle of her arm. Her left arm next, lowering it slightly, creating balance. He touched the small of her back, and she straightened instinctively. Tilted her chin up, just a fraction. Shifted her weight to one foot, her hip following, creating a line that flowed from the floor upward.

He stepped back.

In the mirror, Emma had transformed.

She wasn't just wearing a dress anymore—she was inhabiting it. The pose gave her a height she didn't have, an elegance she hadn't known she possessed. She looked like a painting. Like something you'd stop and stare at in a museum, trying to understand how the artist had captured something so alive.

The three of them stood in silence, looking at her reflection.

Alex became aware, slowly, that Jaime and Emma were both staring at him now instead of the mirror. He felt heat rising to his face.

"What?"

"Alex." Jaime's voice was strange—hushed, almost reverent. "What was that?"

"I just... I saw a painting once. A Degas. She reminded me of it, so I just..." He trailed off, unable to explain what had felt so natural a moment ago and now felt exposed, too intimate, like he'd shown them something he should have kept hidden.

Emma turned from the mirror. Her eyes were bright. "That was the most incredible thing anyone's ever done for me."

"It was just a pose."

"It wasn't just a pose." Jaime was still looking at him with that strange expression. "That was... you closed your eyes and you became someone else. Like you went somewhere."

Alex didn't know what to say. He had gone somewhere—the same place he always went when he was drawing, that quiet space where everything made sense and his hands knew what to do without being told. He just hadn't realized anyone could see it from the outside.

"I'm buying this dress," Emma announced, breaking the moment. "And I'm never posing for a photo again without you."

· · ·

THE COLOGNE COUNTER was Jaime's idea.

"Everyone has a signature scent," he explained as they drifted toward the men's department. "Something that becomes associated with you. When people smell it, they think of you."

"Like how my grandma smelled like lavender?"

"Exactly. Only hopefully less grandma-ish."

The counter was overwhelming—dozens of bottles in various shapes, names Alex didn't recognize, a salesperson hovering nearby with professional interest. Jaime grabbed a small jar from the display and held it out.

"Smell this between fragrances. Clears your palate."

Alex sniffed. "Coffee beans?"

"It resets your nose. Otherwise everything blurs together."

That made sense, actually. Alex breathed in the bitter scent—not unlike the black coffee he drank every morning—and let Jaime spray something on a paper strip.

"What do you think?"

It smelled like... something. Woody, maybe? Alex didn't have the vocabulary. "It's fine?"

"Fine." Jaime looked personally wounded. "This is Armani Code. It's not 'fine.'"

"Okay. It's... good?"

"You're hopeless."

But Jaime was smiling, and they went through six more fragrances anyway, Alex offering variations of "fine" and "good" and "that one's kind of strong" while wondering why they couldn't just go get a pretzel.

"Can I help you find something?"

The salesperson had appeared—young, well-dressed, confident in a way that reminded Alex of Jaime. He was looking at the two of them with a knowing smile.

"We're trying to find his signature scent," Jaime said, gesturing at Alex. "But he's being difficult."

"Aren't they always?" The salesperson laughed. "My

boyfriend's the same way. I work here and he still won't try anything new." He looked between them, his smile warm. "You two make a cute couple, by the way."

Alex felt his face go hot.

"We're not—" he started.

"Oh, thank you!" Emma appeared from nowhere, draping herself between them. "I tell them that all the time. Adorable, right?"

The salesperson laughed and moved on. Alex shot Emma a look.

"What?" She blinked innocently. "He seemed nice."

Alex noticed that Jaime had gone quiet. Not upset—just thoughtful. Like he was turning something over in his mind.

"Pretzels," Alex said firmly. "Now."

THEY FOUND a bench near the fountain, sharing pretzel bites as the sky deepened toward purple. Shoppers drifted past. Music played from somewhere distant.

"Where did you learn to do that?" Jaime asked. "The thing with Emma."

Alex shrugged. "I didn't learn it anywhere. I just... see things. Shapes, positions. When I'm drawing, I can tell when something's off, when the composition doesn't flow. It's the same thing, just in reverse. Instead of drawing what I see, I arranged what I saw to match what I wanted to draw."

He was aware of how strange that sounded.

"You see the best version of things," Jaime said quietly. "That's what you do, isn't it? You look at something—or someone—and you see what they could be. The version most people miss."

Alex went still.

No one had ever said anything like that to him before. Not his parents, who loved him but didn't understand his art. Not his teachers, who praised his technique without seeing what lay beneath it. Not even Jason, who appreciated everything about Alex but had never put it into words like this.

The idea that Jaime saw this in him—recognized it as something essential, not just a skill but a part of who he was—

Something expanded in Alex's chest. A warmth he didn't have a name for.

"I don't know," he finally managed. "I never thought about it that way."

"Well." Jaime's voice was soft. "Now you can."

They sat in silence for a moment, the fountain splashing behind them. Alex was acutely aware of Jaime beside him—the warmth of his shoulder almost touching Alex's, the smell of whatever cologne he'd tested last still clinging faintly to his skin.

He thought about the salesperson's assumption. You two make a cute couple.

He thought about how well Jaime and Emma got along—like two peas in a pod, he'd thought earlier. How it would make sense for them to be together.

But watching Jaime today—the way he moved through the store, the things he knew, the easy comfort he had in spaces Alex found foreign—Alex wasn't so sure anymore.

What kind of guy knew all that about fashion? About scents and undertones and how to pose someone for a photograph?

Was Jaime... that way?

Alex didn't even know what "that way" meant, exactly. Didn't know why the question had surfaced or what he was supposed to do with it. But something in him was paying attention now—noticing something he couldn't quite put his finger on.

The shuttle back to campus was quiet. Emma dozed against the window. Jaime stared out at the passing lights.

Alex stared at nothing, thinking.

. . .

AT HARRISON HALL, they said their goodnights. Emma hugged them both and bounced off toward her dorm. Jaime and Alex climbed the stairs together, parting at the second floor landing.

"Thanks for coming," Jaime said from above.

"Thanks for inviting me."

"See you tomorrow?"

"Yeah. Tomorrow."

Alex went to his room. Closed the door. Sat on his bed in the dark.

You see the best version of things.

The words kept echoing. The way Jaime had looked at him when he said them—like he was seeing something in Alex that Alex had never seen in himself.

He wondered if anyone had ever done that for Jaime.

He wondered a lot of things, suddenly. Questions he didn't have answers for, about a person he was only beginning to understand.

The room was quiet around him. The watercolor on the wall caught the faint light from outside, the one familiar thing in a world that kept shifting into new shapes.

He lay back on his bed and stared at the ceiling, listening to his own breathing, waiting for the questions to settle into something he could name.

They didn't.

5

A Friendly Reminder

Brad McPherson was not used to feeling out of his depth.

On the court, he knew exactly where to be, when to move, how to read the play before it happened. In the weight room, at practice, in the chaos of a game—he was in control. That was his world. That was where he made sense.

Sitting across from Mindy at the Bluestone Grill, watching her pick at a Caesar salad while his ribeye cooled in front of him, he felt none of that certainty.

The restaurant was nicer than their usual spots—white table-cloths, real candles, prices that made him wince. He'd suggested it because Mindy had been complaining lately about always eating at the same places, and he figured a nice dinner might smooth things over. Put her in a good mood. Get her to stop bitching for a while.

It was working, sort of. She seemed pleased with the atmosphere, at least. And she hadn't mentioned the UCA championship or her sorority drama in almost twenty minutes, which was practically a record.

"Did I tell you I texted with Alex the other day?"

Mindy's fork paused halfway to her mouth. "Alex? You still talk to him?"

"Yeah, I talk to my friend." Brad let the word land with enough weight to remind her where the line was. She'd never really understood his friendship with Alex—or Jason, for that matter. To her, they were part of some other Brad, some version of him that didn't fit the image she'd helped construct.

"Sorry, I just meant—" She softened, recognizing the tone. "Didn't he go somewhere for school? Not Duke, obviously."

"Oakwood. Some small place. He says he likes it."

"Mmm." She returned to her salad, interest already fading.

Brad cut into his steak. "We didn't text long, but he said he's doing okay. Making friends, I guess."

"Good for him."

"Yeah." Brad chewed for a moment. "I dunno. I just worry about him sometimes. He never really had a girlfriend, you know? And now he's at this new place where he doesn't know anyone. I was his only real friend besides Jason." He shrugged. "I just hope he's not, like, lonely or whatever."

Mindy set her fork down.

"Brad." She was looking at him with an expression somewhere between amusement and disbelief. "You know Alex is gay, right?"

She said it the way you'd confirm someone's hair color. Not a revelation—a correction. As if Brad had just said he hoped Alex would find a nice girl, and she was gently pointing out why that wasn't going to happen.

Brad's knife stopped mid-cut.

"What?"

"Alex." She tilted her head, studying him. "He's gay. You... you didn't know?"

Brad set his knife down. The restaurant noise seemed to recede—the clinking glasses, the murmured conversations at nearby tables.

"You're serious."

"Oh my God." Mindy's eyes widened, and then—to Brad's clear irritation—she started to laugh. Not at Alex. At Brad. At the sheer absurdity of her boyfriend being this oblivious. "Brad. Seriously? It's like Alex we're talking about. I don't even know him that well, and I've known since sophomore year. Everyone has."

"Everyone."

"Everyone." She dabbed at her lips with her napkin, clearly enjoying his confusion more than she should. "I mean, no one cares. It's not a big deal. My brother's gay—you hang out with him all the time."

Brad leaned back in his chair, his ribeye forgotten. His mind was racing through years of memories, reframing conversations, moments, things Alex had said or hadn't said. All those times he'd asked about girls and Alex had deflected. The way he never seemed interested in the parties where everyone was hooking up. How he'd rather stay home and draw than go to homecoming.

"Why didn't he tell me?"

Mindy's expression softened. For all her sharp edges, she could read Brad better than anyone, and she could see this had genuinely thrown him.

"Maybe he doesn't know himself yet," she said. "Or maybe he's scared. People have all kinds of reasons for not coming out, babe. It doesn't mean he doesn't trust you."

"But I'm supposed to be his friend. I've known him since we were kids."

"And you still are." She shrugged slightly. "I mean, I've never really understood why you two are so close—you're not exactly... similar. But that doesn't change just because you didn't know this about him."

Brad shook his head slowly, still processing. "God. All the stupid shit I've said over the years. The jokes. The—" He couldn't even finish the thought. Every time someone on the team had called something "gay" as an insult. Every casual slur thrown around in the locker room. Every time he'd laughed along or said nothing.

He'd never thought about it. It was just how guys talked.

But Alex had been there for some of those moments. Alex had heard him.

"Hey." Mindy reached across the table and took his hand. Her voice was gentler now, the performative bitchiness set aside. This was the Mindy that only Brad got to see—the one underneath all the polish and ambition. "You can't beat yourself up over stuff you didn't know. We've all said dumb things. It doesn't make you a bad person."

"I should call him. Tell him I know, and it's okay, and—"

"No." Mindy squeezed his hand firmly. "You shouldn't. If he hasn't told you, then it's not your place to bring it up. That's his to share when he's ready."

"So what am I supposed to do?"

"Just... be his friend, I guess. Same as always." She waved her fork vaguely. "Let him know you're there for him or whatever. And if he ever does tell you, act like it's no big deal." She paused, then added with a slight edge: "I mean, it isn't. I don't know why you're making this into a whole thing."

Brad looked at her for a long moment. Sometimes Mindy surprised him. Underneath the scheming and the social climbing, there was actual wisdom. Actual kindness, even if she kept it hidden most of the time.

"How do you know all this?"

"I told you. My brother." She released his hand and picked up her fork again. "He didn't come out until junior year, but I knew way before that. I just waited. Let him figure it out on his own time. And when he finally told me, I acted surprised and support-ive, and that was that."

"You acted surprised?"

"Of course. He needed to feel like it was his moment, his reve-lation. Not something everyone already knew." She pointed her fork at him. "Same thing applies here. When Alex tells you—if he tells you—you let him have that moment. You don't steal it by letting on that you already knew."

Brad nodded slowly. It made sense, even if it felt wrong to just... wait. To not do anything. He wanted to fix it, to make it right, to protect Alex the way he always had.

But this wasn't something he could fix. This was something Alex had to work out for himself.

"Okay," he said finally. "I'll wait."

"Good." Mindy smiled and returned to her salad. "Now eat your steak before it gets cold. Do you know how much that thing cost?"

Brad picked up his knife, but his appetite was gone. He cut a piece mechanically, chewed without tasting.

Alex was gay.

It explained a lot, actually. Things he'd never quite understood suddenly made sense. The way Alex always seemed to be holding something back. The distance that had grown between them in high school, even as Brad tried to stay close. The look on Alex's face sometimes when the guys on the team would talk about girls—not disgust, exactly, but something carefully neutral. Guarded.

Alex had been hiding. For years. And Brad hadn't seen it.

He wondered what else he didn't know about Alex. What other things had he missed while he was busy with basketball and Mindy and being the guy everyone expected him to be?

Maybe they'd grown apart more than he'd realized. Maybe Alex had stopped confiding in him years ago, and Brad just hadn't noticed. All those times they'd hung out, built forts as kids, played video games, talked about the future—had Alex been holding back even then? Had Brad ever really known him at all?

The thought settled heavy in his chest. Not disappointment —nothing like that. More like... doubt. About himself. About what kind of friend he'd actually been.

But he didn't want that. Didn't want to accept that they'd drifted so far apart that Alex couldn't tell him something this important. He wanted to be Alex's friend. A real one. Not just someone from his past who used to matter.

He'd do better. He didn't know how yet, but he'd figure it out.

"Hey," Mindy said, pulling him back to the present. "You okay?"

Brad looked across the table at her. At this restaurant he couldn't really afford, at this life they were building together—practice schedules and sorority events and the assumption that everything would unfold according to plan.

"Yeah," he said. "I'm okay."

He wasn't sure if that was true. But he'd figure that out, too.

6

The Professor

The figure drawing studio smelled like turpentine and old wood.

Alex had found it on his second day—wandered into the Humanities building between classes and followed the scent of linseed oil down a back hallway until he reached a room with north-facing windows and a circle of ancient oak easels. The kind of room that felt like it had been waiting for him.

Now, two weeks into the semester, it was his favorite place on campus. Professor Able ran the class like a workshop rather than a lecture—minimal talking, maximum drawing, the scratch of charcoal and chalk the only soundtrack. The professor himself was exactly what you'd expect: wire-rimmed glasses, closely trimmed beard, corduroy jacket with patches at the elbows, the kind of bowtie that suggested he'd been tying it the same way for forty years.

"Right," Professor Able said, clapping his hands once. "Put your things down. Grab your chalk. Get comfortable at your easels."

The dozen students shuffled into position. Alex settled onto his stool at the two o'clock position, the spot he'd claimed on the first day and returned to ever since. Something about the angle of light from the window felt right.

"Today's exercise is different." The professor moved to the center of the room, hands clasped behind his back. "I want everyone to close their eyes and think of a person you've recently met. Someone new in your life. A classmate, perhaps. Someone you've seen around campus. Anyone."

A few students exchanged uncertain glances.

"You'll draw them from memory. Eyes closed—at least to start. No peeking at your paper. Let your hand follow your mind, not the other way around."

"How are we supposed to know where our lines are?" someone asked.

"You'll figure it out."

"But what if we can't connect—"

"Let your mind feel rather than think," the professor said. "This exercise isn't about producing a masterpiece. It's about learning to trust the connection between your brain and your hand. The image is already inside you. Your job is to let it out."

More uncertain looks. A few students shrugged and picked up their chalk, clearly treating this as an easy day—no grade meant no pressure. Others looked like they were calculating how late they could drop the course.

Alex looked at Professor Able and caught a slight wink.

He picked up his chalk. Closed his eyes.

And the room fell away.

This was the thing Alex had never been able to explain to anyone—not his parents, not Jason, not his high school art teachers. When he drew, really drew, something shifted. The world outside went quiet, and he entered a space that felt more real than reality. Not a place, exactly. A feeling. Like slipping underwater, everything muffled and weightless, his hand moving through currents he couldn't see but could somehow sense.

In the darkness behind his eyelids, a face began to form.

Blond curls catching light. The angle of a jaw. Eyes that seemed to hold something back, even when they were smiling. The slight curve of lips about to speak—or laugh, or say something that would surprise you.

Alex's hand moved across the paper. He didn't think about the lines he was making, the pressure of chalk against newsprint. He just followed the image, tracing the shape of what his mind was showing him.

The high cheekbones. The way the light fell differently on one side of the face than the other. The expression—not quite a smile, but something warmer than neutral. Something that felt like it was looking back at him.

He lost track of time. Lost track of the room, the other students, the scratch and shuffle of chalk around him. There was only the face taking shape under his hand, growing more defined with each stroke, each shadow, each careful gradation of tone.

"Please finish up with what you have. It's almost time for class to end."

Professor Able's voice pulled him back like a hand on his shoulder. Alex blinked, his eyes struggling to adjust to the light. His hand was resting on the easel, chalk still between his fingers. He felt the way he always felt after one of these episodes—slightly disoriented, like waking from a vivid dream.

He looked at his drawing.

And went very still.

Staring back at him from the newsprint was a face rendered in rich, confident strokes of charcoal. The chiaroscuro was striking—deep shadows giving way to luminous highlights, the kind of tonal range that most students spent years trying to achieve. The eyes had depth, reflection, life. The slightly parted lips suggested someone about to speak. The overall effect was less like a sketch and more like a window into another room, where someone real was looking back.

Someone specific.

Alex's breath caught in his throat.

It was Jaime.

Not a generic face that happened to resemble him. Jaime—every detail, every angle, captured with an accuracy that felt almost invasive. The way his hair curled just above his left eyebrow. The particular shape of his mouth when he was about to smile. The expression in his eyes that always seemed to be holding something back.

Alex had drawn Jaime from memory. With his eyes closed. In a room full of people.

And the drawing was... beautiful. Intimate. The kind of portrait you'd make of someone you knew deeply, someone you'd studied for hours, someone you—

He flipped the paper over before he could finish that thought.

"Mr. Robertson."

Alex jumped. Professor Able had appeared beside his easel, moving with the quiet stealth of someone who'd spent decades navigating roomfuls of students.

"May I?" The professor gestured toward the easel.

Alex's face burned. "It's not—I mean, it's just—"

"May I?"

There was no judgment in the professor's voice. Just curiosity, and something else Alex couldn't quite identify. He stepped aside, and Professor Able turned the paper back over.

For a long moment, the professor said nothing. He studied the drawing with the same intensity he brought to critiquing Renaissance masters—head tilted slightly, eyes moving across the composition, taking in details Alex hadn't consciously put there.

"You drew this with your eyes closed," he said finally. It wasn't a question.

"Yes, sir."

"The entire thing?"

"I opened them at the end. To... finish."

Professor Able nodded slowly. "Do you know this person? The subject?"

Alex's throat felt tight. "He's... a friend. From my dorm."

"A friend." The professor's tone was neutral, unreadable. "You've captured him quite completely, for a friend."

Alex didn't know what to say to that. He stared at the floor, at his own shoes, anywhere but at the drawing or the professor's face.

"Mr. Robertson." Professor Able's voice softened. "Look at me, please."

Alex forced himself to meet the professor's eyes.

"I've been teaching figure drawing for thirty-two years. I've seen thousands of students come through this room, most of them talented, many of them dedicated. What you've done here—" he gestured at the drawing "—is not something I can teach. This comes from somewhere else. Somewhere inside you that most people never access."

Alex felt his face grow hotter. "I just drew what I saw. In my head."

"Yes. Exactly." Professor Able turned back to the drawing. "When I look at this, I don't just see technical skill—though the technique is remarkable. I see... intention. Feeling. I see the subject as you see him. Which means I'm seeing something of you, as well."

The words landed somewhere in Alex's chest and stayed there, heavy and warm.

"What I can teach you," the professor continued, "is to trust that. To trust yourself, as an artist. You create from within, Mr. Robertson. The technique will develop—it's already developing. But this?" He tapped the edge of the paper gently. "This is the part that matters. This is your soul on paper."

Alex didn't know how to respond. No one had ever talked about his art this way before—like it meant something beyond just being good at drawing. Like it revealed something about who he was.

"Thank you," he managed.

Professor Able nodded, then moved on to the next student, leaving Alex alone with his drawing.

He looked at Jaime's face staring back at him from the paper. At the care he'd taken, unconsciously, to capture every detail. At the expression in those drawn eyes—something tender, something knowing.

Why Jaime?

The assignment had been to draw someone you'd recently met. Alex had met a few people since arriving—Emma, Carlos, Maya, faces from various classes whose names he barely remembered. Any of them could have surfaced.

But his mind, left to its own devices, had gone straight to Jaime. Had rendered him with a precision and attention that felt almost... reverent.

What did that mean?

Around him, students were packing up, chattering about lunch plans and weekend parties. Alex carefully removed the drawing from his easel and slid it into his portfolio, handling it more gently than he usually handled his work.

He'd figure out what it meant later.

Or maybe he wouldn't.

Maybe he didn't want to. Because that felt like stepping toward something he couldn't see the edges of—something that might be bigger than he was ready for. And Alex had never been the kind of person who embraced that sort of recklessness. He didn't leap without looking. He didn't open doors without knowing what was on the other side.

Some things were better left alone.

. . .

THAT NIGHT, Alex sat on his bed with the drawing spread across his lap.

He'd told himself he wasn't going to look at it again. Had shoved the portfolio under his desk when he got back to his room and tried to focus on homework.

Dinner with Jaime hadn't helped.

It had become routine over the past couple of weeks—meeting at the dining hall around six, grabbing trays, finding a table by the windows. Nothing planned, nothing discussed. It just happened, and then kept happening, until Alex started expecting it without realizing he'd started expecting it.

Tonight, though, he'd been somewhere else entirely. Pushing food around his plate, giving one-word answers, his mind circling back to the drawing no matter how hard he tried to steer it elsewhere.

"You okay?" Jaime had asked, halfway through his second plate of pasta.

"Yeah. Just tired."

"You sure? You've been staring at that chicken like it owes you money."

Alex had forced a laugh, said something about a long day, steered the conversation toward Jaime's geometry class. But he'd felt Jaime watching him for the rest of the meal—that quiet attention, like he was trying to read something Alex wasn't saying.

Now, alone in his room, Alex sat on his bed with the drawing spread across his lap.

He could admit, in the silence, what he hadn't been able to admit in class: this was the best thing he'd ever made. Not because of the technique—though that was there too—but because of something else. Something alive in it.

Professor Able had called it his soul on paper.

Alex wasn't sure about that. But he knew the drawing felt different from anything he'd done before. More honest, somehow. Like he'd accidentally told a truth he hadn't meant to tell.

He looked at Jaime's face—the curve of his mouth, the light in his eyes, the expression that seemed to see right through him even rendered in charcoal on newsprint.

What the hell was going on with him?

He shoved the drawing back into the portfolio. Shoved the portfolio under his desk. Sat there staring at the wall, willing his mind to go somewhere else, anywhere else.

This was the part he hated—the way his brain wouldn't leave things alone. The way it kept circling back, poking at things that were better left untouched. He'd always been able to distract himself before, to bury the uncomfortable stuff under homework or drawing or just... not thinking about it. That had always worked.

It wasn't working now.

He flopped back on his bed and stared at the ceiling.

Just one night. That's all he wanted. One goddamned night where his brain wasn't constantly playing footsie with Jaime.

Was that really so much to ask?

PART II

AWAKENING

7

Coming Closer

The hill had been Jaime's discovery.

"Come on," he'd said after dinner, steering them away from the usual path back to Harrison Hall. "I want to show you something."

Alex had followed without question—partly because he was too tired to argue, partly because following Jaime had become the easiest thing in the world. They'd walked past the student union, past the athletic fields, down a narrow path that cut through a stand of trees until they emerged on a grassy slope at the edge of campus.

"Look up," Jaime said.

Alex did. And forgot, for a moment, how to breathe.

Away from the lampposts and dorm windows, the sky had opened up. Stars everywhere—not the handful he was used to seeing back home, but thousands, scattered across the darkness like someone had flung a jar of glitter at black velvet. The Milky Way stretched overhead, a pale river of light he'd only ever seen in photographs.

"It's incredible," he said, and meant it.

They'd laid down in the grass without discussing it, side by side, shoulders almost touching. The ground was damp with early autumn dew, the cold seeping through Alex's jacket, but he barely noticed. The sky was too big, too full of light, to care about anything else.

That had been two hours ago. Maybe more. Alex had lost track of time somewhere between Orion and the silence.

"Alex?"

"Yeah?"

"Can I ask you something?"

He turned his head slightly, though he couldn't really see Jaime's face in the dark. "You just did."

"Smartass." But Jaime's voice was softer than usual—the performed confidence stripped away. "I mean a real question."

"Sure."

Silence stretched between them. Long enough that Alex started to wonder if Jaime had changed his mind. Then:

"Do you ever daydream? About... important stuff?"

"I think everyone daydreams."

"No, I mean—" Jaime shifted beside him. "Do you ever daydream about being someone you're not? Or maybe... being someone you want to be, but can't?"

The question landed heavier than Alex expected. He stared at the stars, letting it settle, turning it over in his mind the way he turned over everything—slowly, carefully, from every angle.

"I'm sorry," Jaime said after a moment. "Never mind. It's stupid."

"No—I'm just thinking. I do that. Give me a minute."

"Take your time."

Alex appreciated that. Most people filled silences, rushed to the next thing. Jaime just waited.

"I think I understand what you mean," Alex said finally. "Like... everyone sees one version of you, but there's another version underneath? One they don't know about?"

"Yes." Jaime sounded relieved—like he'd been bracing for Alex to tell him the question was stupid. "Exactly like that."

"Then yeah. I do."

Neither spoke for a while. The crickets filled the space between them, a steady pulse in the darkness.

"Can I tell you something?" Jaime asked. "But you have to keep it to yourself."

"Okay."

"I came to Oakwood because..." He stopped, started again. "Everyone thinks I'm this social person, right? Life of the party. Always knows what to say. And I am that, mostly. But underneath..."

Alex waited.

"I'm kind of a homebody. Believe it or not. Everyone assumed I'd go to Columbia—my mom went there, half my high school went there, it's like twenty minutes from our apartment. And I just..." He exhaled. "I couldn't. I needed to get away from all of it. From everyone who already thinks they know who I am."

"Are your parents pressuring you?"

"No, that's the thing. They're great. They didn't even blink when I told them I wanted to come out here—and they'd never heard of Oakwood, didn't understand why I'd want to leave New York for Ohio of all places. But they helped me anyway." Jaime paused. "I think that almost made it harder. If they were pushing me, at least I'd have something to push against. But they're just... supportive. And I still needed to leave."

"Why?"

"I don't know exactly. That's the honest answer. I just felt like I couldn't figure out... whatever I need to figure out... with everyone watching. Does that make sense? I don't even know what I'm looking for. I just know I couldn't find it there."

Alex understood more than Jaime probably realized.

"Jaime?"

"Yeah?"

"I think it's cool you're a homebody. Because I am too."

Alex could feel Jaime relax beside him—a tension releasing that he hadn't even noticed was there.

"Really?"

"Really."

They lay in silence again, but it felt different now. Warmer, somehow, despite the damp grass and the autumn chill settling around them.

"I daydream sometimes," Alex said, surprising himself, "about people not getting me. Like, my parents know me and love me, but they don't really *know* me. You know? Even Jason—he's my best friend, and there's stuff I've never..." He trailed off, unsure how to finish.

"I think I understand."

"Sometimes I feel like no one really sees me. Like I'm the only one who knows there's more underneath. And I don't even know what that 'more' is. I just know it's there." He didn't know why he kept talking. Maybe the darkness made it easier.

"You know that watercolor in my room? The one by my desk?"

"The farmhouse," Jaime said.

"Yeah." Alex picked at the grass beside him. "It was just an assignment in eighth grade, and everyone else just did it to get it done. And I was going to do the same thing, but then I actually tried. I don't even know why. It was just a farmhouse from some old magazine."

Jaime was quiet beside him. Listening.

"And I was proud of it. Which I know sounds dumb, because nobody else cared. It hung on the wall for a week and came down like everything else." He shrugged. "But I don't know, when I finished it, I felt like maybe I was good at something. Or like I knew what I wanted to do. Or... I don't know. I can't really explain it. It just felt important."

"That's not dumb," Jaime said.

"It kind of is, though. Getting all worked up over a painting of a house."

"You kept it."

"Well... yeah. I guess." Alex felt his face warm. "I don't know. It's weird."

"It's not weird."

He pulled another blade of grass just to have something to do with his hands. "Forget it. I don't even know why I brought it up."

But he knew why. He'd just told Jaime something he'd never told anyone — not even Jason, not really. And now he wanted to disappear into that grass.

"Alex?"

"Yeah?"

"I hope I can be here so you're not the only one."

The words hit him somewhere deep—somewhere he hadn't known was unguarded. He felt his eyes sting, and he was grateful for the darkness. At least Jaime couldn't see the tear that slipped down his temple into the grass.

He took a breath. Steadied himself. "Thank you," he managed. "I really... I really appreciate that."

Jaime didn't say anything. Didn't need to. They just lay there, side by side, watching the stars wheel slowly overhead, and Alex felt something shift inside him. Some wall he'd built without realizing it, developing a crack.

He should probably be worried about that.

He wasn't.

AFTER THAT NIGHT, things changed.

Not dramatically—there was no moment Alex could point to and say *that's when it happened.* It was subtler than that. A gradual deepening, like a photograph slowly coming into focus.

They still ate breakfast together most mornings, still walked to Western Lit, still studied in their corner of the library. But now there was something underneath those routines. An awareness. A shorthand that hadn't existed before.

Jaime would catch Alex's eye across the dining hall and raise an eyebrow—*rough morning?*—and Alex would shrug in response—*you have no idea*—and somehow that was a whole conversation. Alex would make some dry observation during Professor Lyden's lecture, barely audible, and Jaime would have to bite his lip to keep from laughing. They'd fall into step without thinking about it, their rhythms synchronized in a way that felt both natural and strange.

Alex noticed things now. Small things. The way Jaime's hair fell across his forehead when he was concentrating on his geometry homework. The specific sound of his laugh—different from his public laugh, softer, less performed. The warmth of his shoulder when they sat close together—closer than Alex sat with anyone else.

He noticed, and then he noticed himself noticing, and then he tried very hard to stop.

It wasn't working.

"You're quiet today," Jaime said one afternoon. They were on a bench outside the library, killing time before their next classes, and Alex had been staring at the same spot on the sidewalk for five minutes.

"Just thinking."

"About what?"

About you, Alex thought. *About why I can't stop thinking about you. About what the hell is happening to me.*

"Nothing," he said. "Just tired."

Jaime studied him for a moment—that look he had, like he could see right through whatever Alex was pretending. But he didn't push. He never pushed. That was the thing about Jaime: he always seemed to know when to let something go.

"Want to get coffee?"

"Sure."

They walked to the campus café, falling into step without trying. The afternoon was crisp and bright, leaves starting to turn at the edges, and Alex found himself hyperaware of the space between them. The few inches of air that separated his arm from Jaime's. How easy it would be to close that gap.

He didn't.

But he thought about it.

THAT NIGHT, back in his room, Alex pulled the drawing out from under his desk.

He'd been doing this more often—taking it out, studying it, trying to understand what his subconscious had been trying to tell him. The face staring back was still Jaime: the careful rendering of his features, the expression in his eyes, the something underneath the surface that Alex had captured without meaning to.

You've captured him quite completely, for a friend.

Professor Able's words echoed in his memory. He'd known, hadn't he? Known what Alex was only beginning to admit.

What was he feeling? He could try to name it—attraction, connection, something more—but the words felt inadequate. This was bigger than vocabulary. This was something that had been building for weeks, maybe longer, maybe his whole life, and now it was refusing to stay buried.

He was coming closer to something. To some truth about himself he'd spent years avoiding.

And the terrifying part was: he wasn't sure he wanted to stop.

He put the drawing back under his desk, face-down. Climbed into bed. Stared at the ceiling.

On the hill that night, Jaime had said he hoped he could be there so Alex wasn't the only one.

Alex was starting to wonder if Jaime already was.

8

First Kiss

It was only supposed to be a few minutes.

The day had been brutal—back-to-back classes, a quiz he'd forgotten about, two hours struggling with a philosophy reading that seemed designed to make him feel stupid. He'd already been fading when Jaime looked up from the table in the library they'd settled into over the past couple of months.

"You look like hell."

"Thanks."

"I'm serious. Let's just head back to my place. It's quieter anyway." Jaime was already packing up his books. "I'll grab us dinner. You can take a nap or something."

"I don't need a nap."

"Uh-huh."

The weather had already turned. Autumn was in full force, but tonight felt like a preview of winter—down in the forties, the kind of cold that cut through you. And of course Alex hadn't worn more than his standard uniform: a light jacket that did nothing against the wind. He shivered the whole way across campus.

Jaime, being from New York, knew how to dress for weather and still look good doing it. He shook his head as Alex's teeth chattered.

"You're freezing."

"I'm fine. It's still warm enough."

"You're literally shivering."

"That's just... exercise. From walking."

Jaime muttered something under his breath—something about having to take care of this boy even if he wouldn't do it himself—and picked up the pace.

"I could just go to my own room," Alex grumbled as they climbed past the second floor. "It's right there."

Jaime ignored him and kept walking up to the third floor. As soon as they were inside his room, he grabbed the hoodie hanging nearest the door and practically forced it over Alex's head.

"Hey—" Alex swatted at him. "I said I'm fine—"

"You're not fine. You're an idiot who doesn't own a real coat. Arms up."

Alex wasn't used to being looked after like this. He'd always taken care of himself, brushed off concern, insisted he was okay even when he wasn't. But as Jaime tugged the hoodie down and stepped back to inspect his work, Alex felt something loosen in his chest. The hoodie was warm, and soft, and smelled like Jaime —that mix of cologne and laundry detergent and something else underneath. It was... nice. Being fussed over. Even if he'd never admit it.

"Better," Jaime said. "Now lie down. I'm going to grab dinner. Take a nap—you need it."

"I don't need—"

"Alex."

"Fine."

Jaime left, and Alex sat down on the bed. The purple comforter was soft. The desk lamp cast a warm glow. He'd just close his eyes for a second while he waited...

And then nothing.

Now he was waking up slowly, drifting up through layers of sleep, aware of warmth and softness and something else he couldn't quite identify. A weight across his chest. A presence behind him. The sound of someone else breathing.

His eyes opened.

Morning light filtered through the blinds. He was still in Jaime's room—he recognized the ceiling, the angle of the window —but something was different. Something was—

There was an arm around him.

Alex went very still. His brain, still foggy with sleep, tried to piece together what had happened. He was still wearing Jaime's hoodie—and he was lying on his side, and behind him, pressed close against his back, was Jaime.

Spooning him.

Alex's heart started to pound. Was this really happening? He didn't know what this was, but it was something, and he should probably—

Jaime stirred. The arm around Alex tightened briefly, then relaxed. And then Jaime made a soft sound—half sigh, half murmur—and Alex felt his breath against the back of his neck.

He didn't move.

He should move. He knew he should move. But his body wasn't listening to his brain anymore. His body was cataloging sensations: the warmth of Jaime's chest against his back, the weight of his arm, the rhythm of his breathing. The way it felt to be held like this—like something precious, something worth protecting.

No one had ever held him like this before.

Alex closed his eyes and let himself have it. Just for a moment. Just until Jaime woke up and the spell broke and every-thing became awkward and complicated. Just this one moment of—

"Alex?"

Jaime's voice was rough with sleep. Alex felt him shift, felt the arm around him loosen as Jaime became aware of their position.

"Yeah?"

"Did we... I mean, I didn't..." Jaime was struggling to form sentences. "You were passed out when I got back with food, and I didn't want to wake you, and there's literally nowhere else to sleep in this stupid tiny room, so I just... I thought I'd stay on my side, but I guess..."

"It's okay."

"Is it?" Jaime sounded uncertain in a way Alex had never heard before. "I didn't mean to—I mean, I just fell asleep and then I woke up and we were—"

"Jaime." Alex turned over carefully, slowly, until they were facing each other on the narrow bed. Inches apart. Close enough that he could see the sleep creases on Jaime's cheek, the way his hair was flattened on one side. "It's okay."

Jaime's eyes met his. Neither of them seemed to know where to look.

"Did you..." Jaime started, then stopped. Tried again. "I mean, are you... is everything..." He winced. "Sorry, I don't know what I'm trying to say."

Alex didn't either. His brain was stuck on how warm Jaime had felt against his back, how safe, how *right*—and now he was terrified that his face was giving all of that away. What if Jaime thought he was weird? What if this ruined everything?

"I'm not upset," Alex said quickly. "If that's what you're asking."

"You're not?"

"No, I just..." He trailed off. What was he supposed to say? *I liked it? I didn't want it to stop? I'm embarrassed that I liked it so much?*

Jaime looked equally lost. "I didn't mean to make things weird. I just—when I woke up and realized we were—I didn't

70

know if you'd be..." He couldn't seem to finish a sentence. "I thought maybe you'd be mad. Or freaked out. Or..."

"I'm not."

"Okay." Jaime nodded, but he still looked uncertain. Like he wanted to ask something else but couldn't figure out how. "So we're... okay?"

"Yeah. We're okay."

They were both quiet for a moment. The morning light was getting brighter, slanting across the bed, catching the gold in Jaime's hair. Alex was suddenly very aware of how close they were. Of the space between them—barely any space at all.

"Alex..."

"Yeah?"

Jaime didn't answer. He just looked at Alex with an expression that was equal parts terrified and hopeful, and Alex felt something shift in his chest. Some barrier he'd been holding up for weeks, maybe years, starting to crack.

He didn't think about it. Didn't let himself think. He just leaned forward—or maybe Jaime leaned forward, or maybe they both did at the same time—and then their lips were touching.

It lasted maybe two seconds. Maybe three.

Then they both pulled back at the same time, eyes wide.

"I'm sorry," Jaime said immediately. "I didn't mean to—I don't know why I—"

"No, I'm sorry, I think I—"

"That was my fault, I shouldn't have—"

"I didn't mean to make you—"

They were both talking over each other, words tumbling out in a rush of panic. Alex's heart was slamming against his ribs. What had he just done? What had *they* just done? He'd never kissed anyone before, never even come close, and now he'd just—with Jaime—and what if Jaime hated him now, what if this ruined everything—

"Please don't hate me," Jaime said, and his voice cracked. "I've never done anything like that before and I don't know what happened and I'm so sorry if I—"

"I don't hate you." Alex could barely get the words out. "Do you hate me?"

"What? No. Why would I—"

"Because I kissed you."

"I think I kissed you."

"I think we kissed each other."

They stared at each other. Both breathing hard. Both terrified.

"I've never done that before," Jaime whispered. "Kissed anyone."

"Me neither."

Silence. The kind that felt like standing on the edge of a cliff, not sure whether to jump or step back.

"Was it..." Jaime started, then stopped. Swallowed. "Did you... I mean... was it okay? That we..."

Alex didn't know how to answer that. His brain was still short-circuiting, still trying to process what had just happened. But underneath the panic, underneath the fear, there was something else. Something that felt like—

"Yeah," he said quietly. "It was okay."

Jaime let out a breath—half laugh, half exhale—the kind of sound you make when you've been holding your breath and realize you're not in trouble after all. Alex heard himself make the same sound, and then they were both laughing nervously, the tension cracking just enough to let them breathe.

The laughter faded. They looked at each other.

Really looked.

Alex could see Jaime searching his face, and he knew he was doing the same thing—not because he didn't trust what Jaime had said, but because he wasn't sure he trusted himself. Was it really okay? Was *he* really okay? Did he even know what okay meant anymore?

Jaime's eyes held the same question.

THEY DIDN'T GET out of bed right away.

There didn't seem to be any rush. Classes could wait. Breakfast could wait. The whole world could wait while they figured out what had just happened—what was still happening, as they lay facing each other on Jaime's narrow bed, knees touching, fingers intertwined between them.

"Can I ask you something?" Alex said.

"You just did."

"Smartass."

Jaime grinned. It looked different this close—more real, less performed. "What do you want to ask?"

"Have you ever... I mean, before me... did you ever think about..."

"Kissing a guy?"

Alex nodded.

Jaime was quiet for a moment. His thumb traced circles on Alex's palm, a gesture that seemed almost unconscious. "Honestly? I don't know. I never really thought about kissing anyone. Not seriously. And then I met you and..." He trailed off, shook his head. "I can't explain it. There was just something. From the first day."

"Seriously?" Alex couldn't help the smile spreading across his face. "You wanted to kiss me then?"

Jaime's cheeks flushed. "No—I mean, yeah—well, I don't know. I didn't know what it was. But there was... something."

"Something," Alex repeated, teasing now.

"Shut up." But Jaime was smiling too. Then his expression shifted, curious. "What about you? Did you... I mean, was this a surprise? Or did you feel it too?"

Alex felt his own face heat up. "I don't know. I never really thought about... any of this. Romance or..." He couldn't even say the word. "...or anything like that."

Jaime looked incredulous. "Really? Everyone thinks about that stuff."

"Not really. I mean..." Alex stared at a spot on the pillow. "I know everyone thought I was weird. Still do, I guess."

"You're not weird."

"I am."

"Well, then so am I, babe."

Alex's eyes snapped up. "Babe?"

Jaime's face went red. "That just—it slipped out. I didn't mean—"

"Where did that come from?"

"Nowhere. Forget it." Jaime was squirming now. "I'm not saying another word because I'm just going to say something stupid."

"Come on." Alex poked his shoulder. "What?"

"No."

"Tell me."

"No way."

Alex poked him again, and Jaime swatted his hand away, and then somehow they were wrestling on the narrow bed, Alex trying to tickle the answer out of him while Jaime laughed and squirmed and tried to fend him off.

"Just tell me!"

"Never!"

Alex managed to pin Jaime's wrists above his head, both of them breathless and grinning. Jaime looked up at him, hair mussed, cheeks flushed, still laughing—and something shifted.

Alex leaned down and kissed him.

This time, they both knew it was coming. This time, they were both ready.

It was longer than before. Slower. Alex felt Jaime's lips soften against his, felt him lean up into the kiss, felt his own body respond in ways he'd never experienced. Jaime's wrists slipped free and his hands found Alex's back, pulling him closer, pulling him down until Alex's full weight was pressing him into the mattress.

Jaime had never felt anything like it—the warmth, the weight, the *closeness*. He couldn't get enough. His fingers tangled in Alex's shirt, tugging him closer still.

Alex played with Jaime's hair as they kissed, tilting his head to find a better angle, something deeper, more urgent. The bottle had been opened and neither of them wanted to stop. Needed more.

Jaime finally tilted his head back, gasping for air, and Alex's lips found his neck, trailing up to his ear, teeth grazing the sensitive skin there—

Jaime made a sound he'd never made before. A place he didn't know about himself.

"Oh god—" He was breathing hard, his whole body electric, hyper-aware of everywhere they were touching—including where Alex was pressed firmly against his thigh. "Maybe we should—"

Alex's lips paused against his neck.

"—slow down?"

Alex inhaled deeply and let out a long, shaky breath. He laughed softly, dropping his forehead to Jaime's shoulder. "You're probably right."

"I really don't want to be right."

"Me neither."

They stayed like that for a moment, catching their breath, hearts pounding against each other. Then Alex lifted his head, looked down at Jaime with a grin, and kissed him quickly on the lips.

"Babe," he said.

Jaime laughed, caught. "Babe."

9

We Love You

The call came somewhere between campus and the state park.

Alex was driving, windows cracked, the October air cool against his face. Jaime had his feet up on the dashboard—a habit Alex would normally hate, but somehow didn't mind when it was Jaime—scrolling through his phone when it buzzed with an incoming call.

"It's my dad." Jaime glanced at Alex, then answered. "Hey, Pop."

Alex kept his eyes on the road, but he could hear the warmth in Thom's voice through the speaker—animated, affectionate, the easy banter of people who actually liked each other. Jaime laughed at something, made a joke about his mom's latest event planning crisis, asked about his dad's students at the studio.

"Yeah, everything's good here. Classes are fine. Weather's actually nice for once." A pause. "No, I'm not on campus. Taking a little road trip with a friend."

Alex felt Jaime glance at him.

"Just to a state park. Nothing crazy." Another pause, longer this time. Jaime's voice shifted slightly—still light, but with something underneath. "Yeah. I will. Okay. Love you too, Dad."

He hung up and set the phone in the cupholder.

Alex waited a beat. "Love you too?"

"What?"

"You said 'love you too.' To your dad. On the phone."

Jaime shrugged. "Yeah. We always say that."

"Huh."

"What, you don't?"

Alex didn't answer. He wasn't sure what to say. His family wasn't the "I love you" type. They showed it in other ways—his mom making his favorite dinner when he came home, his dad helping him change a tire without being asked. But saying it out loud? That wasn't how the Robertsons operated.

"It's just how we are," Jaime said, looking out the window. "My parents are... I don't know. Affectionate, I guess."

Alex nodded, not wanting to push. Jaime had that look—the one that meant there was more underneath, but he wasn't ready to share it yet. Alex was learning to recognize that look. Learning when to wait.

They drove in silence for a few minutes. Fields rolled past, golden and brown in the autumn light. Then Jaime reached over and rested his hand on Alex's leg.

Just resting. Testing.

Alex felt the warmth of it through his jeans. Felt something stir in his chest. Without thinking, he took his right hand off the wheel and found Jaime's fingers, intertwining them.

They drove like that. Watching the road. Feeling each other's presence. Not needing to fill the silence with words.

Jaime was looking out the window when he started talking. Not looking at Alex. Just watching the countryside blur past.

"My mom's kind of amazing, you know? She runs this event planning company in the city. High-end stuff—galas, fundraisers, corporate things. She knows everyone. Remembers everyone's names, their kids' names, what they ordered at dinner three years ago. It's like a superpower."

Alex listened.

"I get that from her, I think. The social thing. Being able to talk to anyone." Jaime paused. "But my heart... that's from my dad."

His hand squeezed Alex's without seeming to realize it.

"He used to be a dancer. Ballet. Pretty well-known in Europe, back in the day. Now he runs a studio, teaches. And he's just... he's the kindest person I've ever met. Never pushes. Always listens." Jaime's voice softened. "When I was in high school, there was this one time—I was maybe fifteen, sixteen—and I was freaking out about something stupid. I don't even remember what. And he just sat with me. Didn't try to fix it. Didn't tell me I was being dramatic. Just said, 'You can be whoever you are, Jaime. Whoever that turns out to be. We'll love you regardless.'"

Alex felt the weight of that. The gift of it.

Then Jaime went quiet.

Alex gave his hand a slight squeeze. Not sure if it was helping, but wanting Jaime to know he was there. Jaime looked over at him, then back out the window.

"There's something I never told you," he said. "About why I really came to Oakwood."

Alex waited.

"In tenth grade, there was this guy. Marcus. He was in my history class, and I just..." Jaime exhaled. "I had the biggest crush on him. Like, couldn't think straight, wrote his name in my notebook like a middle schooler, the whole embarrassing thing."

Alex could picture it—all that energy and emotion focused on a crush.

"And one day, I don't know what I was thinking, but I told him. Just blurted it out after class. Said I liked him. Like, *liked* him."

"What happened?"

"He laughed." Jaime's voice was flat. "Not in a mean way, at first. Just surprised, I think. But then he told his friends, and they thought it was hilarious, and by the end of the day, the whole school knew that Jaime Stamford had a crush on Marcus Chen."

Alex's chest tightened.

"I tried to backpedal. Said it was a joke, a prank, whatever. But nobody believed me. And then..." Jaime's hand squeezed harder. "The school called my dad because Marcus's parents had called them. They were concerned about their son being"—Jaime made air quotes with his hands—"'targeted.'"

Alex could imagine it now—Jaime at sixteen, sitting in the principal's office, his whole world crumbling. His heart sank. He felt for that younger version of Jaime, felt like the hand he was holding was a lifeline connecting that scared kid to the present.

"What did your dad say?"

"He just... asked what happened. Quietly. And I panicked. Denied everything. Said I'd said it but it was all a joke. Tried to make it go away." Jaime wiped at his eye with his free hand. "But I could tell he didn't believe me. He knew. He's always been able to tell when I'm lying."

"Did he push?"

"No. That's the thing. He just said he loved me. That I was at an age when things were confusing, and it was okay to not have everything figured out. And then he let it go."

Alex felt warmth hearing this, but there was something more coming. He could feel it.

"I almost told him," Jaime said. "Right then. Almost said, 'Dad, I think I might be...' But I couldn't. I was too scared. And I didn't even know what I was scared of, because I *knew* he'd still love me. I knew it. But something just... froze."

He went quiet again. Watched the world pass by outside the window.

"I came to Oakwood to start over. That part was true. But really..." His voice cracked. "I didn't want to disappoint him. My dad. I know that doesn't make sense, because he's never been anything but supportive, but I just... I felt like if I told him, something would change. Like he'd look at me differently. And I couldn't handle that."

The tears came then. Quiet, but real.

Alex saw the next exit and took it. Pulled into the back of a truck stop, away from the other cars. Turned off the engine.

Then he turned and pulled Jaime into his chest.

He didn't say anything. Didn't try to fix it or explain it away. Just held him. Let him cry against his shoulder. Let the silence be what it needed to be.

After a while, Jaime started to pull back, embarrassed. "Sorry, I didn't mean to—"

Alex stopped him. Gently. Leaned over and kissed him—quick, tender. Not passion. Just presence. Just love.

Then he helped wipe the tears from Jaime's cheeks.

Jaime caught his eyes. Held them.

"I want to tell my dad," he said quietly.

Alex nodded.

"I want to tell him about... about you." Jaime looked at him like he was asking permission. Like he was terrified of the answer. "That you're my..." He couldn't quite get the word out. "...my b-boyfriend?"

He said it like a question. Like he needed to know if it was true.

Alex didn't freak out. Didn't pull away. Didn't feel the panic he might have expected. Instead, he felt humbled. That Jaime saw him this way. That someone wanted to be with him enough to say that word out loud.

"Okay," Alex whispered.

Jaime blinked. "Okay?"

"Okay."

They sat with that for a moment. Then Jaime said, "That's it? Just 'okay'?"

Alex bit his lip, thinking. He wanted to say more than okay. Wanted to find words that matched what he was feeling. But he'd never been good with words—not spoken ones, anyway.

"I'm scared shitless," he finally said. "Of telling my own dad anything like this. I can't even..." He shook his head. "But your dad. He sounds... I don't know. Good. Like, actually good." He paused, trying to find the right words. "And he already knows, right? I mean, he didn't push back then because he was waiting for you. So maybe..." Alex trailed off, then tried again. "He raised you to trust him. And you do. So maybe just... do that?"

He winced slightly. "Sorry. I'm not good at this."

Jaime was looking at him with something like wonder.

"I'm only eighteen," Alex continued. "We both are. I don't have a clue how any of this works. All I know is I love you and I'll be here to help however I can."

He didn't realize what he'd said until he saw Jaime's eyes widen.

"You... you love me?"

Alex replayed his words. Heard himself say them. *I love you.*

He could backtrack. Say he meant it like friends love each other. Like brothers. That would be true, in a way. But sitting here in this truck stop parking lot, holding Jaime's hand, looking into his tear-streaked face, Alex knew that wasn't the whole truth.

"I don't..." Alex started, then stopped. Started again. "Look, I already said I don't know what I'm doing, and I'm just gonna keep saying that because it's true." He rubbed the back of his neck. "But when I said it—the love thing—I wasn't just... I meant it. I don't know what that means exactly. I've never..." He exhaled. "I'm pulling this out of my ass, but I know how I feel. Even if I can't explain it. You know?"

Jaime practically threw his arms around him. "I love you too," he said into Alex's shoulder. "God, I love you too."

They held each other awkwardly across the center console, and it was clumsy and uncomfortable and perfect.

When they finally pulled apart, Alex said, "We've only been... whatever we are... for a little while. It feels fast to say we're *in love*."

"Yeah," Jaime agreed. "Maybe we're just... following our hearts?"

"Following our hearts." Alex smiled slightly. "I can work with that."

"And I love that we can talk like this. Even when we have no idea what we're doing."

"Especially when we have no idea what we're doing."

A silence settled between them. Not comfortable, exactly. Not resolved. But okay. They didn't have answers. They didn't need them yet.

Jaime suddenly opened his door. "I need a soda. Want anything?"

"Sure."

Alex watched him walk toward the truck stop, his gait lighter than before. He thought about what had just happened. No big dramatic scene. No grand declarations. Just two people figuring things out together. Saying words they'd never said before and trying to understand what they meant.

He'd told Jaime he loved him. And Jaime had said it back.

Alex knew he was still growing up. Still learning who he was. But this moment—this ordinary, extraordinary moment in a truck stop parking lot—felt like something he'd remember forever.

He looked in the rearview mirror and saw Jaime walking back, phone tucked between his shoulder and ear, two sodas in his hands. Alex reached over and unlocked the passenger door.

Jaime tumbled the sodas onto the seat, still talking. His voice was different now—brighter, more open. Alex caught fragments of the conversation.

"...yeah, we just stopped for a drink. I've been talking with my..." A pause. Alex saw Jaime take a breath. "...my boyfriend."

Alex's eyes widened.

Jaime let the word sit there. Then kept going.

"Dad, I need to tell you something. About that day in tenth grade. With Marcus." Another pause. "I should have told you then. I was scared, and I didn't know why, because I knew you'd still love me. But I was." Jaime's voice steadied. "Dad, I'm gay. I should have said it years ago."

Alex felt the words land in his own chest. Hearing them out loud—Jaime saying them to his father—made something shift.

He couldn't hear Thom's response, but he saw Jaime's eyes filling with tears again. He reached over and rubbed Jaime's arm, then took his hand. Jaime smiled at him through the tears and kept talking.

More words Alex couldn't quite make out. Then: "I will, Dad. I love you too."

He hung up.

Sat there for a moment, phone in his lap, tears streaming down his face.

Alex stayed quiet. Present.

"I told him," Jaime said finally. His voice was strange—awed, almost. "That's the first time I've ever said that word out loud. To anyone."

Alex looked at him. Felt the lump in his own throat.

"I told him about you," Jaime continued. "And he said..." He had to stop, compose himself. "He said to tell you he's looking forward to meeting you. And that he's happy for both of us."

Something released in Alex's chest. A tension he hadn't known he was holding.

"That's really great news, babe," he said softly.

Jaime smiled, still crying. Alex reached over to wipe his cheeks.

"Why the tears? This is good, right?"

"I don't know." Jaime shook his head. "I feel like this was supposed to be this whole big thing, you know? And I'm just sitting here in bumfuck Ohio—sorry, no offense—"

Alex shrugged. "None taken."

"—and he acted like he always knew. Like it was nothing."

"He probably always has."

"Yeah. I guess." Jaime looked out the window at the truck stop, the highway beyond, the endless fields. "I just... I wish I were home right now. You know?"

Alex understood then. The tears weren't sadness. They were something else entirely.

Sharing something this big—this beautiful, this life-changing —with someone you love, but doing it on the phone, hundreds of miles away... that was lonely. No amount of words could change that. No amount of "I'm proud of you" could replace being held by your father in that moment.

Sometimes tears weren't things to be wiped away. Sometimes they just needed to be felt.

Alex squeezed Jaime's hand and said nothing.

They sat there together in the parking lot, watching trucks come and go, until Jaime finally wiped his eyes and said they should get going. Adventure awaited.

He meant the state park.

Alex knew it was much more than that.

10

Homecoming

Jason had never driven this far alone.

Two hours didn't sound like much, but sitting behind the wheel of his mom's Honda, watching the familiar streets of Oxford give way to open highway, it felt like crossing into another country. The radio kept him company—some pop station that faded in and out as he moved between signal ranges—and he'd already gone through half the snacks his mom had insisted he pack.

She'd been hesitant about the whole thing. He could tell by the way she'd stirred her leftover spaghetti the night before, not quite looking at him as he made his case.

"It's just a couple hours, Mom. I'll be fine."

"I know you will. I just..." She'd trailed off, and he knew what she was thinking. He was seventeen. This was the longest he'd ever driven on his own. And she was letting him go.

The tipping point had been when he'd mentioned scouting the campus. "If I'm going to apply to Oakwood next year, I should probably see what it's like, right?" It was a throwaway line—he'd known he was losing the argument and had grasped at whatever might work—but something in her face had shifted. Maybe she was remembering her own college days. Maybe she was just tired of fighting.

"Take your sleeping bag," she'd said finally. "I don't want you getting sick on some cold floor."

Now he was forty minutes out, and his stomach was doing things that had nothing to do with the gas station hot dog he'd eaten an hour ago. He was about to see Alex. Really see him, in his new life, in this new place that had nothing to do with Oxford or high school or any of the history they shared. Alex had mentioned a friend named Jaime a few times—some guy from New York he'd hit it off with—but Jason didn't know much beyond that.

He was excited. He was nervous. He wasn't sure which feeling was winning.

THE CAMPUS WAS SMALLER than he'd expected.

Jason pulled into the visitor lot and sat there for a moment, engine idling, taking it in. Brick buildings covered in ivy. A clock tower in the distance. Students walking in pairs and groups, backpacks slung over shoulders, looking like they belonged here in a way Jason couldn't quite imagine for himself.

He texted Alex: *I'm here. Visitor lot.*

The response came immediately: *Stay there. Coming to get you.*

Jason got out of the car and leaned against the hood, trying to look casual. Trying not to feel like a high school kid playing dress-up in a college world.

Then he saw them coming down the hillside—Alex in the lead, moving with an ease Jason had never seen in him before, and behind him, a guy with golden hair and a smile that seemed to take up half his face.

Jaime. He'd seen a photo Alex had texted once, but seeing

him in person was different. He moved with an easy confidence, like he'd never met a stranger in his life. The kind of person who made you feel like you were already friends.

"Welcome to Oakwood!" Alex called out, grinning. "Ready to leave?"

"I'd staple my balls to a chair before I'd go through that drive every day," Jason said, and immediately wondered if that was too much. But Alex just laughed, and Jaime—

"This is exactly how I met this one," Jaime said, thumbing toward Alex. "Cranky and dramatic."

"I was not cranky."

"You were a little cranky."

"I was overwhelmed. There's a difference."

"That's what cranky people say."

Jason watched them go back and forth. "Jesus, you two sound like an old married couple."

They both stopped. Looked at each other. Something passed between them—a glance Jason couldn't quite read—before they burst out laughing.

"He's got us pegged already," Jaime said.

"Give him five minutes," Alex replied.

Jason filed that look away. He wasn't sure what it meant, but it felt like something.

"C'mon," Alex said, grabbing Jason's backpack before he could protest. You're staying in my room—I'll crash with Jaime tonight." Jason raised an eyebrow but didn't comment. Something to file away.

Alex put his arm around his shoulders and kept it there as they walked up the hillside.

Jason almost teased him—something about Alex going soft, since when was he so touchy-feely?—but then he caught the look on Alex's face and swallowed the joke.

It had only been a couple of months since they'd last seen each other, but Alex was different. More relaxed. Happier, maybe. The guarded tension that had always lived in his shoulders seemed... gone. Jason couldn't help but wonder if college had done this—being away from home, from Oxford, from all of it—or if Jaime had something to do with the change.

"If you're serious about coming here next year," Alex said, "you should see what you're getting into."

Jason nodded, but his mind snagged on the words. Not just the campus. Not just the classes. But this—whatever this was. Alex and Jaime, finishing each other's sentences. Inside jokes Jason wasn't part of. A whole life that had bloomed in the months since Alex had left.

He was happy for Alex. He really was. But there was something else underneath, something he didn't want to look at too closely. A twinge of envy, maybe. Alex was here, blossoming, becoming whoever he was supposed to be. And Jason was still stuck in Oxford, finishing senior year, waiting for his own life to start.

"You okay?" Alex asked, squeezing his shoulder.

"Yeah." Jason forced a smile. "Just taking it all in."

He pulled out his phone and thumbed a quick text to his mom: *Made it. All good.*

"Texting your mom?" Alex asked.

"Promised I would."

"Good." Alex ruffled his hair—that annoying thing he'd been doing since they were twelve. "You know how she gets."

Jason ducked away. "Yeah, yeah."

Jaime was watching them with an amused expression. "You two have known each other forever, huh?"

"Since we were kids," Alex said.

"I have stories," Jason added. "So many stories."

"Oh, I'm going to need those."

"No, you're not," Alex said quickly.

"I absolutely am."

Jason laughed—a real laugh, loosening something in his chest.

Jaime was easy to be around. Warm. The kind of person who made you feel included even when you were clearly the outsider. No wonder Alex liked him.

As they reached the dorm entrance, Jason thought maybe he could fit into this new world after all. Not as the center of it—that spot seemed to belong to someone else now—but somewhere nearby. A part of it, at least.

ALEX'S DORM room was smaller than Jason expected.

Not that his own room back home was anything special, but this felt almost claustrophobic—a narrow bed, a desk crammed into the corner, a window that looked out onto the side of another building. How did anyone live like this?

But it was so *Alex.* Neat, almost spartan. A few books stacked precisely on the desk. Sketchpads tucked into a corner. And on the little nightstand—

Jason moved closer, picking up the small frames arranged by the lamp. The family Christmas photo he'd seen a thousand times. The one of Alex's grandmother, faded and precious. A photo of the three brothers that Jason had actually been there when it was taken.

And then a new one.

It was from a photo booth—the kind you found at malls, the ones that printed strips of four images. Alex and Jaime, making faces in the first shot. Laughing in the second. Looking at each other in the third.

And in the fourth—

Jason blinked. Looked closer.

They were kissing.

He stood there holding the frame, his brain doing something strange. Not the shock he might have expected. Not disgust or confusion. Something else entirely.

Alex had put this photo on his nightstand. Right there where he'd see it before he fell asleep and again when he woke up. Like it was the most natural thing in the world. Like it belonged there.

Everything clicked.

The random texts over the past couple of months—brief, happy, different from the Alex he'd known. The photo of Jaime that Alex had sent just last week, no explanation, just *"This is Jaime"* with a smiley face. The way they'd been finishing each other's sentences since Jason arrived. The glance when he'd called them an old married couple.

This was Alex's boyfriend.

Jason's chest felt tight, but not in a bad way. In a way he didn't have words for. He looked at the photo again—at Alex's face in that kiss, relaxed and happy and *open* in a way Jason had never seen him. And something deep inside Jason ached.

He wanted this.

Not just to be happy for Alex—though he was, he really was —but to have this for himself. To feel that open. To have someone look at him the way Jaime was looking at Alex in that third shot. To be brave enough to put a photo like this on his nightstand where anyone could see.

And underneath that, something else. Something he'd never let himself look at directly.

All those years of quick side hugs. The way his heart would speed up when Alex's shoulder brushed his. The daydreams he'd pushed away because boys in Oxford didn't think about other boys like that. The reason he'd felt so hollow when Alex left for college, a feeling too big to just be missing a friend.

He'd liked Alex. Maybe for years. Maybe always.

And now Alex had found someone else. Someone who could give him what Jason had never been brave enough to name, let alone offer.

Behind him, Alex and Jaime had gone quiet. Jason could feel them watching him.

He turned around slowly.

Alex's face was pale. He looked terrified—more scared than Jason had ever seen him. Like he was bracing for something to shatter.

"Jace, I..." Alex started, then stopped. Tried again. "I was going to tell you. I just didn't know how to—"

"You and Jaime?" Jason's voice came out strange. Thick.

Alex nodded. He looked like he might be sick.

Jason looked at Jaime, who had taken a small step back, giving them space. Then back at Alex. His best friend since forever. The person who knew him better than anyone.

The person he'd been half in love with without ever admitting it.

"How long?"

"A few weeks. It's still..." Alex swallowed. "It's new. We're still figuring it out."

Jason nodded slowly. His mind was racing—not just through memories of Alex, but through everything he'd been pushing down for years. Every time he'd told himself it was normal to think about your best friend that much. Every time he'd ignored the way his stomach flipped when Alex smiled at him.

"Are you..." Alex's voice cracked. "Are you freaked out?"

Jason looked at the photo booth picture still in his hand. At the fourth shot. At Alex's face in that kiss—happy in a way Jason had always wanted to make him but never knew how.

"No," he said finally. And meant it. "I'm not freaked out."

Alex let out a breath like he'd been holding it for years.

"I'm just..." Jason set the frame back carefully. "I'm surprised, I guess. I didn't know you were..." He still couldn't say the word. Couldn't say it about Alex, couldn't say it about himself.

"Neither did I," Alex said quietly. "Not really. Not until I got here. Not until Jaime."

Jason looked at Jaime again. Really looked at him this time—not as Alex's college friend, but as the person who had unlocked something in his best friend that Jason had never been able to reach. That Jason had wanted to reach, even if he'd never admitted it.

"You make him happy?" Jason asked.

Jaime nodded. "I try to."

"Good." Jason turned back to Alex. "Then I'm happy for you, man. Both of you."

Alex's eyes were wet. "Really?"

"Really." Jason crossed the small room and pulled Alex into a hug—a real one, not the quick side-hugs they'd always done because anything more felt too dangerous. He held on tight, and something in his chest cracked open. "You're my best friend. That doesn't change because you're..." He still couldn't say it. "Because of this."

Alex hugged him back, tight. "Thanks, Jace."

When Jason finally let go, his eyes were stinging. He wiped at them quickly, embarrassed.

The room was quiet. Heavy with something unfinished.

Jaime had been watching. Not intruding—just present, leaning against the doorframe with his arms crossed. But his eyes were sharp, taking in more than either of them probably realized.

"Can I say something?" Jaime asked. "And like, tell me to shut up if I'm overstepping, but..."

Alex and Jason both looked at him.

"That was huge. What just happened." He pushed off the doorframe, took a step closer. "Alex, you just came out to your best friend. And Jason—you handled that... I mean, really well."

Jason shifted uncomfortably. "He's my best friend. It doesn't change anything."

"I know. But I also noticed something." Jaime paused, like he was figuring out how to say it. "Neither of you could say it. The word. Gay."

The silence that followed was thick.

"I get it," Jaime continued. "I couldn't either. For years, I was dancing around it in my own head. Couldn't even admit it to myself. And even when Alex and I first..." He gestured vaguely between them. "I still couldn't say it out loud. Like if I didn't say the word, it wasn't real or something." He paused. "But then I did. And it was scary as hell. Like jumping off a cliff." A small, almost shy smile. "But then it felt like I could actually fly. Which sounds stupid, but... I still feel that way."

He looked between them, uncertain. "I don't know if I should be pushing this. It's not my place. But I just... I wanted you both to know that with me, at least, it's okay. Whatever you're feeling. It's okay."

"What was the nudge?" Jason asked quietly. "That made you finally say it?"

Jaime looked at Alex. Something soft passed over his face.

"We were in this truck stop a couple weeks ago in the middle of nowhere and I was looking at him—" He stopped, shook his head like the memory still surprised him. "And I just knew I couldn't keep hiding anymore. I loved him. And I wanted my dad to know. Finally."

Jason blinked. He remembered that photo now—the blonde guy, the big smile, the cryptic caption. *Doing really good. Met a great friend.*

Only Jaime wasn't just a friend. He was Alex's boyfriend.

And Jaime had just said he loved him.

That was huge.

Alex was looking at Jason with an expression that said everything he couldn't put into words. *Sorry I didn't tell you. I just... didn't know how.*

Jason crossed back to him and pulled him into another hug. Longer this time. Tighter.

"I'm sorry," Alex whispered against his shoulder. "I should've told you. I just—"

"Don't apologize."

"But I—"

"Alex. Don't."

Alex was quiet for a moment. Then, barely audible: "Jason... I'm gay." His voice cracked on the word. "I hope... that's okay."

Jason squeezed tighter, then pulled back to look at Alex. Alex might have been a year older, but right now he looked like a kid. Scared. Hopeful. Waiting for permission to exist.

"I sorta knew," Jason said quietly.

Alex's eyes widened.

"I mean—I didn't *know* know. But I..." Jason's voice faltered. "I wasn't sure what I was. What I am. But I think I... I mean, looking back, I think maybe I..."

He couldn't finish. But he turned to look at Jaime, one arm still around Alex.

"I'm a little jealous," he admitted. "Of you. Because I always thought..." He shook his head. "I can't. I don't know how to say it."

Jaime smiled—not mocking, just understanding. He stepped forward and put a hand on each of their shoulders.

"I know," he said. "Alex is a pretty special guy, isn't he?"

Jason's face went red. He looked at the floor.

And Alex—Alex was staring at Jason like he was seeing him for the first time. Like something that had always been in front of him had suddenly come into focus.

"Jace?" Alex's voice was tentative. Surprised.

Jason couldn't meet his eyes.

Alex pulled him in again—tighter this time, and somehow different. Not Jason comforting Alex anymore. The other way around.

Jaime stepped back, giving them room. Watching with a warmth that suggested he'd known exactly what he was doing when he started this conversation. Maybe he hadn't known how it would end. But he'd sensed it needed to happen.

"You're still my best friend," Alex said quietly, his arms wrapped around Jason. "That's not going to change. Just because Jaime and I are together doesn't mean I don't..." He paused. Took a breath. "Doesn't mean I don't love you."

The words landed somewhere deep in Jason's chest.

Alex had never said that before. Not like this. Not out loud.

They both felt the weight of it. Alex seemed almost startled by his own words, but he didn't take them back. Jaime was smiling a few feet away—pleased, like they'd finally gotten past something he'd later call "that midwestern politeness bullshit" and found their way to something real.

Jason's throat was too tight to speak. But he managed, after a long moment:

"I love you too."

He meant it in every way he didn't have words for yet. And Alex seemed to understand that.

They stood there holding onto each other—Alex's chin hooked over Jason's shoulder, Jason's fingers gripping the back of Alex's shirt like he was afraid to let go. Neither of them crying exactly, but close. Jaime watched from a few steps back, giving them the time they needed, his expression soft and knowing.

Some things didn't need to be rushed.

EVENTUALLY, Jaime broke the silence.

"Okay," he said, warmth in his voice. "I think we've all earned some food. And maybe some air."

They headed out into the evening, the three of them. The weight of everything that had happened in that small dorm room followed them for a block or two, but somewhere between the quad and the edge of campus, it started to lift.

"So," Jaime said, glancing at Jason with a mischievous look. "I'm going to need those middle school stories you mentioned earlier."

"Oh, absolutely," Jason said, matching his energy. "Did he tell you about the science fair incident?"

"There was a science fair incident?" Jaime's eyes lit up.

"Nope," Alex cut in. "We're not doing this."

"He tried to build a volcano—"

"Jason, I swear to God—"

"—and it actually erupted. Like, *actually* erupted. All over Mrs. Patterson's desk."

Jaime was already laughing. "Oh my god."

"There was baking soda everywhere. She had to evacuate the classroom."

"I was twelve!" Alex protested.

"You were a menace to society."

"I hate both of you," Alex muttered, but he was fighting a smile.

"No you don't," Jason and Jaime said at the same time. They looked at each other and grinned—a look that said *oh, this is going to be fun.*

And somehow, impossibly, they fell into an easy rhythm. Jason had been worried about being the third wheel, the outsider intruding on their couple bubble. But it wasn't like that at all.

If anything, it felt like Jaime and Jason were the ones teaming up. And Alex was their favorite target.

LATER THAT NIGHT, Jason lay on Alex's narrow bed staring at the ceiling.

Alex had gone to Jaime's room. The dorm was quiet. Unfamiliar sounds—pipes settling, distant laughter, someone's music through the walls—but somehow not unsettling.

He felt safe here. He didn't know why.

Maybe it was the room itself. Small, spartan, so completely Alex. Or maybe it was what had happened in it. The things he'd said. The things he'd finally let himself feel.

He wasn't ready to say the word yet. Not even in his own head. But something had shifted. A door had cracked open—just a sliver—and light was coming through. And he knew, without them, he never would have gotten this far.

He thought about Alex saying *I love you*. The first time anyone outside his family had ever said that to him. And he'd said it back. And meant it.

He thought about Jaime—how he'd pushed, gently, in exactly the right way. How he'd known what to say and when to step back.

He thought about going home tomorrow.

Back to Oxford. Back to high school. Back to the version of himself that didn't ask questions or look too closely.

Even as he thought it, he was already planning the next trip. Maybe in a few weeks. Maybe sooner. The drive wasn't that bad after all. He could make it again.

He would. He wanted to. Because he missed Alex. He missed... this.

11

Unraveling

The letter arrived on a Tuesday.

Elizabeth Robertson sorted through the mail the way she always did—standing at the kitchen counter, one eye on the oven where Scotty's after-school snack was warming. Bills went in one pile. Junk mail went straight to recycling. Anything that looked important got set aside for her husband's desk.

The envelope from Oakwood University gave her pause.

Dear Parent/Guardian, it began.

She skimmed the first few lines, her lips moving slightly as she read. Something about a Parent's Weekend. A welcome reception. Dinner. A cocktail hour.

Cocktail hour.

Elizabeth's stomach tightened. She wasn't a drinker—never had been—and the thought of standing in a room full of strangers with wine glasses made her feel vaguely ill. Her usual social world consisted of church potlucks and the occasional neighborhood cookout. Events where she knew everyone, where the conversation stayed comfortable, where people believed the same things she did.

This felt different. Formal. The kind of place where she'd have to make small talk with professors and other parents—people from cities, probably. People who might look at her and see... what? A small-town woman who didn't belong?

She folded the letter back into its envelope and set it on the desk alongside the other letters.

THAT EVENING, after the boys were fed and Scotty was parked in front of the television, Bill called her into his office.

"What's this about a Parent's Weekend?"

Elizabeth stood in the doorway, arms crossed over her chest. "It came in the mail today. I wasn't sure if we should go."

He had his reading glasses on, scanning the invitation. "Looks like a dinner. Reception beforehand. They've already assigned us seats." He squinted at something handwritten at the bottom. "Table 22." He set the letter down and looked up at her. "You don't sound enthusiastic."

She shifted her weight. "It's just... it's a lot. Driving all that way for a dinner with people we don't know. And there's a cocktail hour, Bill. I don't think—"

"It's probably just finger foods and mingling. Like those conventions I go to in Columbus."

"You go to those alone. I've never—" She stopped herself, but the point was made.

Bill set the letter down and looked up at her. "I know it's outside your comfort zone, Liz. But I'd like to see how Alex is settling in. Talk to some of the other parents, maybe. Get a little more involved." He pulled off his glasses and rubbed the bridge of his nose. "I only saw the campus for a few hours when we did that visit over the summer. This would be different—actually seeing him in his element."

Elizabeth didn't answer right away. The truth was, she wasn't sure she wanted to know what Alex was up to. He'd been different on their last phone call—lighter, somehow. Happier. He'd mentioned a friend named Jaime more than once, and something about the way he said the name made her uneasy in a way she couldn't quite articulate.

"I suppose," she finally said.

"Good. It's settled then." Bill was already reaching for the desk phone. "I'll give him a call and let him know we're coming."

THE PHONE RANG JUST as Alex was leaving for dinner.

He almost let it go to voicemail—he was supposed to meet Jaime in ten minutes—but something made him glance at the screen. *Home.*

His stomach dropped.

"Hey, Dad."

"Hey, sport. How's it going?"

"Good. Fine. Classes are good."

The small talk felt stiff, the way it always did with his father. Alex paced his small room, phone pressed to his ear, waiting for whatever this call was actually about.

"Listen," Bill said, "we got that letter about the Parent's Weekend dinner. Your mother and I are planning to come."

Alex stopped pacing.

Parent's Weekend. He'd gotten a note about it weeks ago—something about a cocktail reception and dinner, parents mingling with faculty. He'd glanced at it and tossed it aside. His parents weren't the type to attend cocktail receptions. He'd just assumed they wouldn't bother making the drive.

"Oh," he managed. "Really?"

"It's a week from Friday. We'll drive over for the dinner and head back that night—can't leave Jimmy and Scotty for too long. But we wanted to check in. See how you're settling in. Meet some of the other parents."

"Right. Yeah. That sounds... good."

"Everything okay, son? You sound a little off."

"No, I'm fine. Just surprised. I didn't think you guys would want to make the drive."

"Well, your mother took some convincing. But I think it'll be good for us." A pause. "You doing okay? Making friends?"

Alex's throat tightened. "Yeah. I've got a good group."

"That's good. That's real good." Another pause—longer this time. "Alright, well, I'll let you go. Just wanted to give you a heads up."

"Thanks, Dad."

"See you in a couple weeks, sport."

The line went dead.

Alex stood there for a long moment, phone still in his hand, staring at nothing.

His parents were coming.

His mind immediately went to Jaime. His parents would definitely be there—Jaime's mom had probably already booked flights the moment she got the invitation. Jaime's parents at one table, his own parents at another. In the same room. At the same event.

Maybe that was okay? Maybe they just... wouldn't sit together. Parents probably got assigned to their own kid's table, right? He tried to remember what the note had said about seating. Had there been assigned seats? He couldn't remember. He'd barely skimmed it.

God, this was complicated.

He thought about the photo booth picture on his nightstand. The one with the kiss in the fourth frame. He'd have to hide that before they visited his room.

His phone buzzed. A text from Jaime: *you coming? i'm starving*

Alex typed back: *be there in 5. need to talk to you about something*

uh oh. that sounds ominous

not bad. just... complicated

okay now i'm worried. hurry up

Alex grabbed his jacket and headed out. He needed to talk to Jaime. Figure out a plan. Maybe it would be fine—maybe their parents would never even cross paths.

But something in his gut told him it wasn't going to be that simple.

JAIME WAS WAITING outside the dining hall. "What's wrong?" he asked the moment he saw Alex's face.

"Not here."

They grabbed trays and went through the line in silence, Jaime throwing him glances the whole time. Once they found a quiet corner away from the usual crowd, Jaime set down his tray.

"Okay. What's the complicated thing?"

Alex pushed his food around his plate. "My parents are coming. For Parent's Weekend."

Jaime's fork paused midway to his mouth. "Oh."

"Yeah."

"Okay." He set the fork down. "That's... I mean, that's normal, right? Parents come to Parent's Weekend. It's kind of in the name."

"I know. But—" Alex lowered his voice, even though no one was sitting near them. "They don't know. About us. About me. About any of it."

"I know." Jaime's voice was gentle. They'd talked about this before.

"And your parents will be there too, right?"

"Yeah. They already booked their flights."

Alex exhaled slowly. "So we'll all be in the same room. At the same dinner."

"Probably not the same table, though. I'm sure they seat families together."

"Right. So maybe..." Alex trailed off, hating himself for what he was about to say. "Maybe we just... don't introduce them? Like, you stay with your parents, I stay with mine, and we just... get through the evening?"

Jaime didn't say anything for a moment. His expression shifted—not angry, but something underneath. Hurt, maybe.

"So I'd be someone you're hiding," he said quietly.

"No. I mean—" Alex felt sick. "It's only a couple hours. They'll come, we'll do the dinner thing, and then they'll drive home. It's not like—"

"Alex." Jaime set his fork down. "I get it. I do. Your family is... complicated. And I'm not going to push you into something you're not ready for."

"But?"

"But it sucks." Jaime looked at him directly. "Sitting in the same room, pretending we don't know each other. Having to watch what I say, how I look at you, making sure I don't accidentally—" He shook his head. "I did that for years. Hiding. Pretending. And I really don't want to go back to it."

"I know. I don't want that either."

"And my parents know, Alex. They know about us. So I'd be sitting there with them, and they'd know exactly why I'm not coming over to say hi to you. That's..." He exhaled. "That's a lot to ask."

Alex stared at his untouched food. "I'm sorry. I know it's not fair."

"It's not about fair." Jaime's voice softened. "It's your decision. Your family. I'll do whatever you need me to do. But I also don't want to feel like something you're ashamed of."

The words landed hard.

"I'm not ashamed of you," Alex said. "I'm just—"

"Scared. I know." Jaime reached across the table and touched his hand briefly. "I was too. But hiding didn't make it better. It just made it lonelier."

Alex didn't have an answer. He stared at his plate and felt the walls closing in.

"Maybe I could tell them before," he said quietly. "On the phone, or—"

"Hey." Jaime squeezed his hand. "You don't have to figure this out tonight. We've got two weeks."

"Two weeks isn't very long."

"It's longer than you think." Jaime finally took a bite of his salad. "And whatever you decide, I'm with you. Okay? Even if it means being your 'good friend from New York' for one awkward dinner."

Alex managed a small smile. "You'd do that?"

"I'd hate every second of it. But yeah." Jaime shrugged. "That's what boyfriends do, right?"

The word still sent a small thrill through Alex's chest, even now. Boyfriend. He had a boyfriend. Someone who would stand beside him through awkward dinners and impossible conversations and all the messy parts he hadn't figured out yet.

"Thank you," he said.

"Don't thank me yet. You haven't seen me try to act straight. It's not pretty."

Alex laughed—a real laugh, loosening something in his chest. "I'd pay money to see that, actually."

"Oh, it's happening. I'm going to talk about sports and cars and—what else do straight guys talk about? Beer?"

"You don't even like beer."

"I'll pretend. Very convincingly." Jaime grinned. "I'll be like, 'Hey Mr. Robertson, how about those... Buckeyes?'"

"We're not in Columbus. And you don't know anything about football."

"I know they wear helmets. That's something."

Alex shook his head, still smiling. The knot in his stomach hadn't fully loosened, but it was better than before. Manageable.

Two weeks. He had two weeks to figure out how to keep his carefully constructed world from falling apart.

JIMMY CRANKED up the volume on his iPod until Metallica drowned out everything else.

Parent's Weekend. He'd heard his dad on the phone with Alex. Talking about driving all the way to Oakwood for some fancy dinner. For *Alex.* The golden boy. The one who got to escape while Jimmy was stuck here babysitting Scotty and listening to his mom remind him to take out the trash.

Fucking bullshit.

He mouthed the words along with the song, careful not to actually say them out loud. His parents would lose their minds if they knew what was on his iPod. Metallica. Megadeth. Slayer. Anything loud and angry and nothing like the Christian radio station his mom kept on in the kitchen.

That was his thing. His secret rebellion. His folks thought he was their good little athlete—varsity track as a freshman, decent grades, popular with the right kids. They had no idea he knew more swear words than half the seniors. Or that he practiced them on Scotty when no one was around, just to see his brother's eyes go wide.

Tell Mom and I'll give you the worst wedgie of your life, he'd warned him once. Scotty believed it. Smart kid.

Jimmy paused the music and stared at the ceiling.

The thing that pissed him off most? He was doing everything right. Sports. Grades. Friends. He had a plan: keep the grades up, get a scholarship to a Big 10 school, graduate with honors, land a good job, marry someone hot, have a couple kids. Treat them better than he was being treated.

Meanwhile, Alex—quiet, weird, artsy Alex who never played a sport in his life—got to be the one their parents drove hours to see. Got to be the one their dad called "sport" on the phone like he actually gave a shit.

Jimmy shoved his earbuds back in and turned the volume up until his ears hurt.

Fuck Alex. Fuck Parent's Weekend. Fuck all of it.

He'd show them. Someday, he'd be the one they drove hours to see. The one who made something of himself. The one who didn't need their approval because he'd already proven he was better than whatever they thought he was.

12

The Secret

The idea came from Jaime, because of course it did.

"We should go to Oxford."

They were sprawled on Jaime's bed, textbooks open but ignored, the Sunday afternoon sun slanting through the window. Jason had left that morning—hugs in the parking lot, promises to text, the Civic disappearing down the campus road.

Alex looked up from his phone. "What?"

"Oxford. Your hometown. Jason came all the way down here to see you—we should return the favor."

"That's... different."

"How is it different?"

Alex didn't have a good answer. "It just is."

"I want to see where you grew up." Jaime rolled onto his side, propping his head on his hand. "The house. Your old school. That diner you're always talking about."

"I never talk about a diner."

"You mentioned it once. Something about pie."

"That was Jason's thing, not mine."

"Still. I want to see it." Jaime's voice softened. "I want to know that part of you."

Alex stared at the ceiling. The thought of bringing Jaime to Oxford made his chest tight. It wasn't that he was ashamed—he wasn't, not anymore. But Oxford was his parents' territory. His mother's world. The place where he'd spent eighteen years learning to be invisible.

"My parents can't know," he said finally.

"Okay."

"I mean it. If we go, we'd have to... I don't know. Sneak around. Stay somewhere else."

"We could stay with Jason."

Alex considered this. Jason's mom worked weekends sometimes. And Jason had that mostly empty house since his dad left. It could work.

"Let me call him," Alex said, already reaching for his phone.

Jason picked up on the second ring. "Miss me already? I've barely been home an hour."

"Jaime wants to come to Oxford."

A pause. Then, excited: "Wait, seriously? When?"

"Next weekend, maybe? If that works for you."

"Hell yes it works for me." Jason's voice was practically vibrating. "You can stay here. Mom won't care—I'll just tell her Jaime's a friend from school or whatever. When are you getting in? Friday night? Saturday morning? I can show Jaime around, there's this—"

"Jace. Breathe."

"Right. Sorry. I'm just—" A laugh. "This is gonna be awesome."

Alex glanced at Jaime, who was grinning. "Yeah," he said. "I guess it is."

THEY DROVE UP SATURDAY MORNING, arriving just before noon.

Oxford looked exactly the same—which shouldn't have surprised Alex, but somehow did. The same brick buildings downtown. The same church steeples. The same quiet streets where nothing ever happened and everyone knew everyone else's business.

"It's cute," Jaime said, peering out the window.

"It's small."

"That too."

Jason was waiting on his front porch when they pulled up, practically bouncing. He had Alex in a hug before the car door was fully closed, then turned to Jaime with the same enthusiasm.

"Welcome to Oxford! Population: boring."

"I've heard worse reviews."

"Come on, I'll give you the tour. And by tour I mean we'll drive around for ten minutes and then get food because there's literally nothing else to do."

Alex felt something loosen in his chest. This was okay. This was Jason's world—not his parents', not the church's, not the suffocating expectations he'd grown up under. Just his best friend's house, where he could be himself.

For the weekend, at least.

THE TOUR TOOK EXACTLY twelve minutes.

"And that's the high school," Jason said, gesturing out the window as they drove past. "Where dreams go to die."

"Dramatic," Jaime observed.

"You didn't go there."

"Fair point."

They ended up at Jason's house, sprawled across his living room floor with pizza from the place on Main Street—yes, Oxford actually had a Main Street. Jason was telling Jaime about the time Alex had accidentally set off the fire alarm during art class, and Alex was pretending to be annoyed while secretly loving every second of it.

He'd been so worried. About coming here, about Jaime seeing this small-town version of his life, about everything. But sitting here eating pizza for late lunch and laughing and watching Jaime fit in like he'd known them both for years... Alex felt something loosen. His guard slipping. And before he knew what he was doing, he leaned over and kissed Jaime.

Quick. Casual. Natural.

And got pizza sauce on Jaime's nose in the process.

"Oh my god." Alex started laughing. "I'm so sorry—"

Jaime went cross-eyed trying to look at the red smear on his nose, which only made it worse.

"Smooth," Jason said, tossing a napkin at them. "God, you gays are disgusting." He was laughing as he said it.

But inside, he was watching Alex in a way he hadn't before. This was something new—Alex leaning in without thinking, kissing someone like it was the most natural thing in the world. Like he was finally himself.

It only made Jason love him more.

JENN GOT HOME AROUND FIVE.

Jason hadn't told her they were coming. Partly because he wanted it to be a surprise. Mostly because he didn't quite know how to explain who Jaime was.

So when she walked through the front door, tired from her shift, and found three boys sprawled across her living room floor surrounded by pizza boxes, she stopped dead.

"Jason Michael—"

"Surprise?" Jason offered weakly.

But Jaime was already on his feet, crossing the room with that easy confidence of his. "Mrs.—sorry, I don't actually know your last name. I'm Jaime. I'm so sorry we didn't call ahead. This was completely my idea, and I take full responsibility for the ambush."

He extended his hand. Jenn took it, still looking slightly stunned.

"Jaime's a friend from my dorm," Alex blurted out. "From college."

He regretted it instantly. Jaime wasn't his roommate. Why had he said that? But the lie was already out there, hanging in the air.

More like best friend at this point," Jaime corrected.

Jason felt a small twist in his gut. He knew it was just a cover story. But still.

"Alex has told us so much about Oxford, and I just had to see where he grew up. I hope it's okay that we're crashing here. Jason said it would be fine, but if it's an imposition—"

"No, no." Jenn was already softening. It was impossible not to —Jaime had that effect on people. "Any friend of Alex's is welcome here. I just wish someone had warned me so I could've tidied up."

"The house looks great," Jaime said. "Seriously. You should see our dorm room." He caught Alex's eye for a split second—a flicker of *I've got you*—before turning back to Jenn. "Alex is a slob, by the way. Don't let him fool you."

"I am not."

"There are socks everywhere. Everywhere."

The lie settled into place. Alex felt a twist of guilt, but Jaime was already moving the conversation forward, smooth as ever.

Jenn laughed. And just like that, Jaime had won her over.

Jaime started asking about her work, about Jason as a kid, about the town. He had a way of making people feel like they were the most interesting person in the room. Alex watched, quietly proud.

Jenn watched too. More than any of them probably realized.

She noticed how many times Jaime reached for Alex's hand

without seeming to think about it. The way they'd catch each other's eyes and share some private joke. The way Alex leaned toward Jaime like a plant toward sunlight.

They weren't exactly hiding anything, even if they probably thought they were.

She smiled to herself. None of this surprised her about Alex. She'd thought about it over the years—especially given his artistic nature, the way he'd never shown much interest in girls, something she couldn't quite articulate but somehow knew. Or thought she did.

It didn't matter, of course. Alex was Alex. She'd always loved that boy.

But it had made her spend some nights thinking about what it might mean for Jason. Especially after his father left. She wasn't sure how her son was truly coping, and if he was dealing with *this* on top of everything else... well, she didn't know the best way to help. She'd been waiting. Watching. Hoping he'd come to her when he was ready.

And now here was Alex, clearly happy, clearly in love, with this charming boy. And Jason—her Jason—had come back from visiting them last weekend brighter than she'd seen him in a long time.

Whatever was happening here, it was good. She could feel it.

"So," Jaime said, clapping his hands together. "I'm taking everyone to dinner tonight. My treat. No arguments, no bitching —sorry, Mrs.... what is your last name?"

"Mitchell. But call me Jenn."

"Jenn. No arguments, no bitching. I've already decided. You're going to be my date for the evening."

Jenn laughed—a real laugh, surprised out of her. "Well then. I guess I'd better get myself gussied up. Where are we going?"

They debated the options, which didn't take long. Oxford wasn't exactly a culinary destination.

"There's the Italian place on Main," Jason offered. "Or the steakhouse, but that's expensive."

"What about Applebee's?" Jenn suggested.

Jaime's face did something complicated—a flicker of disappointment he almost managed to hide. Alex caught it and bit back a smile.

"Applebee's," Jaime repeated, recovering quickly. "Perfect. I've heard amazing things. Very... authentic American cuisine."

"You're thinking of Olive Garden," Jason said.

"Those breadsticks *are* pretty good," Jenn admitted.

"Applebee's it is!" Jaime declared, as if he were announcing a reservation at a Michelin-starred restaurant. "Let me just freshen up. Jenn, wear something fabulous. This is a *date*, after all."

He disappeared toward the bathroom, and Jenn turned to Alex with raised eyebrows.

"He's... something."

Alex grinned. "Yeah. He really is."

They piled into Jenn's car—Jason in front, Alex and Jaime in the back.

Alex caught himself creating distance—knees not quite touching, hands in his own lap. Old habits. The instinct to hide, even now.

Jaime noticed. Of course he did. His pinky found Alex's on the seat between them. A small rebellion against years of careful camouflage.

It's okay. We're safe here.

Alex let his hand relax. Let their fingers intertwine. Jenn glanced in the rearview mirror and smiled but said nothing.

THE RESTAURANT WAS HALF-EMPTY on a Saturday night, which was typical for Oxford. They got a booth in the corner— Jaime slid in next to Jenn, playing up the "date" bit, while Alex and Jason took the opposite side.

Jaime scanned the menu with exaggerated seriousness. "Okay, we need an appetizer. And drinks." He flipped to the back. "Oh, they have margaritas. You should get one, Jenn. I love margaritas, but—" He stopped himself, glancing down. "Sorry. My mom lets me have a sip sometimes when we're out, but..."

Jenn laughed. "You know what? I think I will. Jason can drive us home." She grabbed Jaime's hand with theatrical flair. "And if my date is nice to me, maybe I'll let him have a taste." She winked at Alex.

Alex felt his face warm. Did she know? The way she'd said *date*, the wink—it felt like she was telling him something.

Jason was watching his mom with an expression Alex couldn't quite read. She hadn't been like this in... he couldn't remember how long. Relaxed. Playful. Like the weight she usually carried had lifted for the night.

It was nice.

By the time the food arrived, Jenn was on her second margarita and laughing at Jaime's stories about New York. She asked questions about college, about their classes, treating them like adults instead of kids to be managed.

"So how did you two become friends?" she asked, gesturing between Alex and Jaime with her fork.

"Move-in day," Jaime said easily. "The parking lot was a disaster—I helped him find a spot. He was standing by his car looking like he was about to bitchslap a nun."

Jenn nearly did a spit-take with her margarita.

"I was *not*—"

"You absolutely were. You had this look on your face like the whole world had personally offended you. I thought you were going to start swinging at the welcome signs."

"I was overwhelmed! It was a confusing parking lot!"

Jenn was still laughing, dabbing at her chin with a napkin. "Oh, I can picture it. That's exactly how Alex gets when he's frustrated."

"Thank you for the support," Alex muttered.

"Honey, I've known you since you were eight. You once threatened to throw your math textbook out a window because you couldn't figure out long division."

"I was *ten*."

"You were dramatic."

Jaime was grinning. "See? I knew I liked you, Jenn."

"You two are good together," she said. Casual. Like she was commenting on the weather.

The table went quiet.

Alex felt his heart stop. Across the table, Jaime went very still. Jason looked between them, eyes wide, like he was watching a car accident in slow motion.

"I mean..." Jenn took a sip of her margarita, watching them over the rim. "I'm not blind, boys."

Alex opened his mouth. Nothing came out. His brain was screaming at him to say something—anything—but the words wouldn't form. He could feel Jason tensing beside him, ready to jump in with some deflection, some save.

But it was Jaime who spoke.

"We're not roommates," he said. His voice was calm. Easy. Like he was asking someone to pass the salt. "That was a lie, and I'm sorry about that. I'm Alex's boyfriend."

Jason made a small choking sound.

Alex sat frozen, shoulders braced like he was waiting to be hit.

Jenn looked at them—at Alex's terror, at Jaime's quiet confidence, at her own son's panic on their behalf—and nearly laughed.

"Oh, honey," she said, shaking her head. The margarita had loosened something in her, but it was more than that. She was genuinely amused. "Did you really think I'd care?"

Alex blinked. "I—what?"

"I've known you since you were a kid, Alex. And I've been

watching you two all night." She lifted her glass. "Good for you. Both of you."

She clinked it against Jaime's water, then reached across to tap Alex's Coke. Jason was staring at his plate, face unreadable.

"I mean it," Jenn continued, her voice softer now. "You deserve to be happy, Alex. And Jaime—" She turned to him with a warmth that made Alex's throat tight. "You take care of him, okay? He's a special one."

"I know," Jaime said softly. "I will."

The rest of dinner passed in a blur. Alex couldn't quite believe what had happened—that Jaime had just said it, that Jenn had laughed, that the world hadn't ended. Under the table, Jaime's foot found his and pressed gently. Alex pressed back.

THE CAR RIDE home was quiet.

Jason was driving, eyes fixed on the road. Jenn was in the passenger seat, humming along to the radio, pleasantly buzzed from her margaritas. Alex and Jaime were in the back, closer this time.

They were almost to the house when Jason spoke.

"Mom?"

"Yeah, honey?"

A pause. Alex watched Jason's shoulders rise and fall with a deep breath.

"I'm gay too."

Jason's hands tightened on the steering wheel. The car didn't swerve, didn't slow down. He just kept driving, eyes fixed straight ahead.

Jenn was quiet for a moment. Then: "Okay."

"Okay?" Jason's voice cracked.

"Okay." She reached over and put her hand on his arm. "I love you, Jason. That doesn't change because of who you love."

In the backseat, Alex wasn't breathing. Jaime's hand had gone tight around his.

Jason made a sound—half laugh, half sob. "That's it? Just... okay?"

"What did you want me to say?"

"I don't know. I thought—" He wiped at his eyes with one hand, still driving. "I thought it would be harder."

"Pull over, honey."

Jason pulled into their driveway—they were almost home anyway—and put the car in park. His hands were shaking.

Jenn unbuckled her seatbelt and turned to face him, reaching across the console to take his hand.

"Jason. Look at me."

He did. His eyes were wet.

"I have loved you since the moment I knew you existed. Nothing—*nothing*—is ever going to change that. Do you understand?"

Jason nodded, tears streaming down his face now.

"Come here."

She pulled him into an awkward hug across the center console, and Alex felt his own eyes stinging. Jaime squeezed his hand so hard it almost hurt.

After a long moment, Jenn pulled back. "Okay. Everyone inside. I think we could all use some ice cream."

LATER, after Jenn had gone to bed, the three of them sat on Jason's bedroom floor.

"Why did you tell her?" Alex asked. "Tonight, I mean. In the car."

Jason hugged his knees to his chest. "I don't know. I just... I saw how she was with you guys. How easy it was. And I thought, maybe..." He shrugged. "I didn't plan it. It just came out."

"I'm proud of you," Jaime said.

"Yeah?"

"Yeah. That took guts."

Jason laughed weakly. "I almost threw up."

"Still counts."

Nobody said anything for a minute. Then Jason's expression shifted—something vulnerable crossing his face.

"Can I tell you guys something?"

"Always," Alex said.

Jason picked at the carpet, not meeting their eyes. "I'm happy for you. Both of you. I really am. But sometimes I wonder if..." He trailed off, shrugged. "I don't know. If I'll ever find that."

"You will," Jaime said.

"How do you know?" Jason's voice was small. "There's no one else gay in Oxford. And even if there was—how would I know? It's not like people wear signs. And even then, they probably wouldn't..." He shook his head. "No one's ever even looked at me that way. Like, ever. I can't even imagine someone wanting to kiss me."

"That's not true," Alex said. "You're—"

"I'm what? A catch?" Jason laughed, but there was no humor in it. "That's what people say when they're being nice."

"I'm not being nice. You're good-looking, you're funny, you're—"

"I've never been kissed, Alex." Jason said it flat. Final. "Seventeen years old and I've never been kissed. I always thought my first kiss would be..."

He glanced at Alex, then quickly away. Face reddening.

"Would be what?" Jaime asked gently.

"Nothing. Forget it."

But Alex understood. Something clicked into place—all those years of friendship, of closeness, of something he'd never quite been able to name. The way Jason had looked at him when he'd said I love you too back in Alex's dorm room last weekend.

"Me," Alex said quietly. "You thought it would be me."

Jason's face crumpled. "I'm sorry. I know that's weird. I know you're with Jaime and I would never—I'm not trying to—"

"Jace." Alex moved closer, put a hand on his shoulder. "It's okay."

"It's not weird," Jaime added. He'd shifted too, and Alex caught the look he gave him. A small nod. Permission.

"Jason," Alex said. "Look at me."

Jason looked up, eyes wet, face a mess of embarrassment and longing and years of wanting something he thought he could never have.

Alex leaned in and kissed him.

It was soft. Gentle. Nothing like the hungry, desperate kisses he shared with Jaime. This was something else—a gift. A first. The thing Jason had been dreaming about since before he knew what the dreams meant.

When Alex pulled back, Jason's eyes were wide. Stunned.

"There," Alex said softly. "Now you've been kissed."

Jason's mouth opened and closed. No sound came out.

"Breathe," Jaime said, amused.

"I—you—" Jason turned to Jaime, panic creeping into his expression. "Are you mad? I didn't mean to—he just—"

"I'm not mad." Jaime was smiling. "That was my idea."

"Your... what?"

"Alex loves you, Jason. I love you too. Not the same way we love each other, but—" He shrugged. "You deserved to have that moment. With someone who cares about you."

Jason looked between them, overwhelmed. "I don't... I don't know what to say."

"You don't have to say anything."

"But what about—I mean, won't this make things weird?"

"Only if we let it." Alex took his hand. "You're my best friend. That's not changing. And now you can stop worrying about your first kiss, because it's done. Check that box."

"With the guy I always imagined," Jason said quietly. Almost to himself.

"Yeah." Alex squeezed his hand. "With me."

Jason laughed—a wet, shaky sound—and then he was crying again, but different this time. Relief, maybe. Release.

Jaime moved closer and wrapped an arm around him. Alex did the same from the other side. The three of them sat there on Jason's bedroom floor, tangled together, while Jason cried out years of loneliness and longing.

"You're going to find someone," Alex said. "Someone who looks at you the way Jaime looks at me. I promise."

"How do you know?"

"Because you're a catch, Jace. Anyone would be lucky to have you."

"He's right," Jaime added. "And when we get back to school, we're going to find you a man. There's got to be someone on campus worthy of you."

Jason laughed through his tears. "You make me sound like a project."

"You're not a project. You're our friend. And friends help friends find boyfriends."

"Is that a rule?"

"It is now."

They stayed like that for a long time—three boys on a bedroom floor, holding each other up. Outside, Oxford slept, unaware that anything had changed.

But something had. For all of them.

SUNDAY MORNING, Jenn insisted on breakfast.

"Waffle House," she announced. "My treat. Nothing but the best for my boys."

Jason groaned from under his pillow. "Mom, it's early."

"It's nine-thirty. Up. All of you."

They piled into the car again—rumpled and sleepy, but smiling. The Waffle House was crowded with the after-church crowd, but they found a booth near the window and ordered too much food.

Jenn was different this morning. Lighter. She kept looking at Jason like she was seeing him for the first time—not with confusion or concern, but with a kind of wonder. Like she was proud of the person he was becoming.

"Thank you," Jason said quietly, halfway through his waffle. "For last night. For being... you know."

"For being your mother?" Jenn smiled. "That's not something you thank me for, honey. That's just what I am."

Alex watched them—the way Jenn touched Jason's arm without thinking, the way they finished each other's sentences—and felt a pang of something complicated. Jealousy, maybe. Or longing. His own mother had never looked at him that way.

Jaime's foot found his under the table. A gentle pressure. *I know. I'm here.*

After breakfast, they stood in the parking lot saying goodbye. Jenn hugged each of them in turn—Alex longest of all.

"You take care of yourself," she said quietly. "And know that you're always welcome here. Both of you."

"Thank you, Mrs.—Jenn."

"I mean it, Alex. Whatever happens with your family..." She pulled back, looked him in the eye. "You have people who love you. Don't forget that."

Alex nodded, not trusting his voice.

They walked toward their cars—Jenn and Jason to hers, Alex and Jaime to the Corolla. Jason hung back for a moment, pulling Alex into one more hug.

"Thanks for coming," he said quietly. "This weekend was..."

"Yeah," Alex said. "It was."

Jason let go, then turned to Jaime. He hugged him too—and then, quick and unexpected, kissed him on the cheek.

"You deserved one too," Jason whispered. "After last night."

Jaime's face broke into a grin, delighted. Alex blinked, surprised—then smiled. Something warm spread through his chest.

Jason jogged to catch up with his mom, glancing back once with a wave. Alex watched him go, then turned toward Jaime.

Without thinking, he reached over and took Jaime's hand.

It felt natural. Right. For just a moment, he forgot where he was.

THE ROBERTSON FAMILY was driving home from Grace Lutheran, same as every Sunday.

Bill was behind the wheel, Liz in the passenger seat, Scotty in the back playing with a toy car. Jimmy sat beside his little brother, earbuds in, staring out the window at the nothing that was Oxford on a Sunday morning.

They stopped at a red light. Jimmy's gaze drifted to the Waffle House parking lot across the street.

And froze.

There was Alex. His brother Alex, who was supposed to be at college two hours away. Walking across a parking lot with some blonde guy Jimmy had never seen before.

Holding hands.

Jimmy blinked. Looked again. They were definitely holding hands—fingers interlaced, casual, comfortable. Like it was nothing.

The blonde guy said something, and Alex laughed. Actually *laughed*—open and happy in a way Jimmy had never seen before. Then they got into a car and drove away.

The light turned green. Bill pulled forward. No one else had noticed.

Jimmy slowly pulled out one earbud, heart pounding.
Holy shit.

He'd suspected, maybe. Somewhere in the back of his mind. Alex had always been different—quiet, artistic, never interested in girls the way Jimmy's friends were. But suspecting and *knowing* were different things.

His brother was gay.

His brother was gay, and he had a boyfriend, and he was sneaking around Oxford without telling their parents.

Jimmy slipped the earbud back in and turned to look out the window again.

Well. That explained a few things.

13

Brothers

Jimmy found Jason in the art room during third period.

He'd noticed him there a few times before—Jason had some kind of free period and always used it to work on his drawings in the empty classroom. Today, Jimmy faked a bathroom pass to get out of Algebra. Told Mr. Hibbert he had diarrhea, which shut down any follow-up questions real fast. Now he was standing in the doorway, watching Jason work on some pen and ink thing, trying to figure out how to start this conversation.

"You busy?"

Jason looked up, surprised. "Uh, aren't you supposed to be in class?"

"I'm using the restroom," Jimmy said, doing air quotes with his fingers. "Officially."

"In the art room?"

"It's a big building. I got lost."

Jason set down his pen and capped his ink jar. They weren't friends exactly—Jimmy was a freshman, Jason was a senior—but they'd known each other forever. Jason had been coming over to hang out with Alex since before Jimmy could remember.

"What's up?" Jason asked.

Jimmy glanced around to make sure they were alone, then walked further into the room. "I saw Alex yesterday. At Waffle House."

Jason's face did something complicated. "Oh."

"With some blonde dude." Jimmy sat on the corner of a desk. "They were holding hands."

Silence.

"I'm not gonna narc or anything," Jimmy added quickly. "I'm not a dick. I just—I didn't know he was in town. And I didn't know he was..." He made a vague gesture.

"Gay," Jason said.

"Yeah. That."

Jason was quiet for a moment. "Did you tell anyone?"

"No. Jesus. I just said I wasn't gonna narc." Jimmy felt irritated now. "What, you think I'm gonna run home and tell my parents? Fuck that."

"Sorry. I just—I'm protective of him."

"Yeah, I get it." And he did, even if it stung a little. Jason had always been more of a brother to Alex than Jimmy had. That was just how it was.

"So you knew," Jimmy said. "About him."

"Yeah."

"For how long?"

"A while."

Jimmy picked at a dried glob of paint on the desk. "Cool. Cool cool cool. So everyone knew except me. That's awesome."

"It wasn't like that. It's his thing to tell. I couldn't just—"

"Whatever. I get it." Jimmy stood up. "The blonde guy. That's his boyfriend?"

Jason nodded. "Jaime. He's a good dude."

"Huh." Jimmy tried to picture it—his weird, quiet brother with a boyfriend. Holding hands in a parking lot like it was nothing. Laughing in a way Jimmy had literally never seen him laugh. "He looked happy."

"He is."

"Good. That's... yeah. Good." Jimmy headed for the door, then stopped. "I'm not gonna say anything. To anyone. Just so we're clear."

"I know you're not." Jason hesitated. "But Alex is going to freak when he finds out you know."

"Tell him to chill the fuck out. I'm not trying to ruin his life or whatever."

Jason almost smiled. "I'll pass that along."

ALEX'S PHONE had been on silent during figure drawing. When he finally checked it between classes, there were messages waiting.

> JACE
>
> hey jimmy came to find me at school
> just now he knows about you and jaime
> don't freak he's cool might reach out

And right below it:

> JIMMY
>
> yo

Alex's stomach dropped. He stared at the screen for a long moment, heart pounding.

> Hey what's up

Three dots. Then nothing. Then dots again.

> nothin
>
> hows school

Something was off. Alex could feel it.

> Good. Busy. You?

boring as shit

hey can i call u later

Alex's stomach dropped.

> Sure. Everything ok?

ya just wanna talk

if thats cool

> Yeah. After 8?

k

Alex sat there for a full minute, phone in hand, his heart still going a million miles an hour. Then he pulled up Jason's message again.

> Just got off the phone with Jimmy

JACE
and?

> says hes not going to tell anyone said hes got my back

told u

> im still freaking out

ull be ok i think he meant it

JAIME FOUND him twenty minutes later, still frozen in the same chair.

"Hey." Jaime slid into the seat across from him. "You look like someone died."

Alex handed over his phone. Watched Jaime's face as he read.

"So Jimmy knows," Jaime said when he finished.

"Jimmy knows."

"And he's not telling anyone."

"That's what Jason says."

"Then what's the problem?"

Alex laughed—a short, sharp sound. "The problem is my fifteen-year-old brother knows I'm gay before I've told him. Before I've told anyone in my family. And now he wants to 'talk' and I have no idea what that means."

Jaime reached across and took his hand. "It means he wants to talk. That's not automatically bad."

"What if he's pissed? What if he feels like I've been lying to him?"

"Have you?"

"I—" Alex stopped. "I don't know. Maybe? I never told him, but I never told him I was straight either. I just... didn't tell him anything."

"So tell him now." Jaime squeezed his hand. "He's your brother. He reached out. That's not nothing."

Alex nodded, but the knot in his stomach didn't loosen.

"You want me there when you call him?"

"No. I think... I need to do this alone."

"Okay." Jaime lifted Alex's hand and kissed his knuckles. "But I'm here after. Whatever happens."

THE CALL CAME at 8:17.

Alex was sitting on his bed, door closed, rehearsing what to say. When Jimmy's name lit up his screen, he almost let it go to voicemail.

But he didn't.

"Hey."

"Hey." Jimmy's voice sounded weird. Younger. "Thanks for, uh. Picking up."

"Yeah. Of course."

Silence. Alex could hear something in the background—music, maybe. Jimmy's playlist that their parents didn't know about.

"So," Jimmy said. "Jason told you."

"Yeah."

"I wasn't trying to spy on you or whatever. We were just driving home from church and I looked over and..." He trailed off. "I saw you. With that guy."

"Jaime."

"Yeah. Him." A pause. "Is he, like... your boyfriend?"

Alex closed his eyes. He could lie. Could say it was a misunderstanding, that Jimmy had seen wrong. But what was the point?

"Yeah. He's my boyfriend."

"Huh." Jimmy was quiet for a second. "Okay."

"Okay?"

"Yeah, okay. What'd you think I was gonna do, lose my shit?"

"I didn't know what you were going to do."

"Well, I'm not gonna tell Mom and Dad, if that's what you're worried about. I'm not a fucking snitch."

"I know you're not."

"Then why didn't you tell me?" Jimmy's voice had an edge now. "Jason knows. Your boyfriend knows. Probably half your college knows. And I'm your brother and I had to find out by accident in a Waffle House parking lot."

"Jimmy—"

"No, seriously. I'm always the last to know anything. It's like I don't even exist in this family." He was on a roll now, the frustration pouring out. "Mom and Dad never shut up about you. It's always Alex this, college that, Parent's Weekend, blah blah

blah. Dad took a whole day off work to drive you to that campus visit thing. He's never come to a single one of my games. Not one."

"I didn't know that."

"Yeah, well. Now you do." Jimmy's voice was bitter. "And the whole time, you've got this whole secret life, and you couldn't even text me about it. I'm just the annoying little brother nobody tells anything."

"That's not—" Alex started, then stopped. Took a breath. "Jimmy, it's not about you. It's not about whether I trust you."

"Then what the fuck is it about?"

"It's about what happens if they find out."

Jimmy was quiet for a second. "What do you mean? What do you think they're gonna do?"

"Think about it." Alex's voice was tight now. "Think about Mom. Church every Sunday. Bible study. All that stuff about how we're supposed to live."

Jimmy didn't say anything.

"What do you think she's gonna say when she finds out her son is—"

Alex didn't finish. He didn't have to.

Jimmy went quiet. Really quiet.

He'd been so pissed about being left out, about everyone knowing except him, that he hadn't actually thought about this part. He hated his parents riding his ass all the time. Hated how everything was always about Alex. But he couldn't imagine them actually doing anything bad to Alex.

Right?

But even as he thought it, he knew. He'd heard the way their mom talked about "those people" when something came on the news. The way their dad changed the channel. The pamphlets from church about "God's design for marriage."

"Fuck," Jimmy said quietly.

"Yeah."

"They wouldn't—I mean—" He stopped. Tried again. "You don't think they'd kick you out or something. Right?"

Silence.

"Alex?"

Nothing. And then Jimmy heard it—a sound that made his chest hurt. Something he hadn't heard since they were little kids. Alex was crying. Not loud, not dramatic. Just quiet, shaky breathing. Trying to hold it together and failing.

"I don't know," Alex finally said. His voice cracked on the words. "I don't know, Jimmy."

That was it. No explanation. No list of fears. Just those three words, broken in half.

And Jimmy got it. All at once, he got it.

He didn't need Alex to spell it out. He knew their parents. He knew how their mom got when the news showed a pride parade. He knew the look on their dad's face. He knew what they believed, what they'd been taught to believe, what they'd taught their kids to believe.

Alex didn't know what would happen. That was the worst part. He had no idea if he'd come home for Thanksgiving and everything would be fine, or if his stuff would be in boxes on the porch.

"That's so fucked up," Jimmy said. His voice came out rough. "Alex, that's really fucked up."

Alex didn't answer. Just kept trying to breathe.

"I'm sorry." Jimmy meant it. "I was being a dick. I was so pissed about being left out that I didn't—I wasn't thinking about why."

"It's okay."

"No, it's not." Jimmy rubbed his face with his free hand. This was way more complicated than he'd thought. Alex wasn't just the golden boy, the one their parents loved more. He was his big brother, alone at college, terrified that his own family might throw him away.

"Hey," Jimmy said. "I'm not gonna tell them. I already said that, but I mean it. Not ever. Not until you're ready."

"Thanks." Alex's voice was still thick.

"And if they—" He stopped, not sure how to say it. "If anything happens. When you tell them or whatever. I've got your back. Okay?"

Silence.

"I mean it," Jimmy said. "You're my brother. That's not gonna change because Mom's got a stick up her ass about church stuff. Fuck them if they can't deal with it."

Alex made a sound—half laugh, half sob. "Jimmy—"

"I'm serious. You're still my brother. That's the rule."

The silence that followed felt different. Heavier. Like something had shifted between them that couldn't shift back.

"Thanks," Alex said finally. His voice was still shaky, but steadier now. "I didn't expect this. From you."

"What, me not being an asshole?"

"Pretty much."

"Yeah, well. Don't get used to it."

They were both quiet for a moment. Alex's breathing was steadier now. Jimmy could hear him pulling himself together on the other end.

"Hey," Alex said. "That stuff you said before. About Mom and Dad. About them never coming to your games."

"Forget it. It doesn't matter."

"It does though." Alex's voice was quiet. "I always thought they liked you better. You were the athlete. The normal one. I was just the weird kid who drew pictures."

"That's bullshit."

"Maybe. But that's how it felt."

Jimmy was quiet. He'd spent years thinking Alex had it made. And the whole time, Alex had been scared shitless.

"We're both kind of fucked up," Jimmy said.

"No shit."

"I mean it though. This whole family is fucked up. You're scared they'll kick you out, and I'm pissed they don't even notice I'm here." He paused. "So does this mean I can make gay jokes now?"

"Absolutely not."

"Too late. I've been saving them up."

"I hate you."

"No you don't."

They sat with that for a moment. The silence felt different now—not awkward, just... full. Like two people who'd finally said the things they'd been carrying around.

"Hey," Jimmy said finally. "Your boyfriend. Jaime. He good to you?"

Alex almost smiled. "Yeah. He's really good to me."

"Okay. 'Cause if he's not, I meant what I said. I'll kick his ass."

"You've never even met him."

"Don't need to. You're my brother. That's the rule."

Something warm spread through Alex's chest. "I'll let him know he's on notice."

"Do that." Jimmy paused. "And Alex?"

"Yeah?"

"You can text me. Or whatever. If you need to talk or just... I don't know. I'm here. Even if I'm shit at this stuff."

Alex swallowed past the lump in his throat. "Thanks, Jimmy. Really."

"Yeah, yeah. Don't make it weird." But his voice was softer now. "I gotta go. Scotty's being a little shit and Mom's yelling about something."

"Okay."

"Later."

"Later, Jimmy."

The line went dead.

Alex sat there in the quiet, phone still in his hand. His face was wet—when had he started crying again?—and his chest felt

138

hollowed out in a strange, good way. Like something heavy had been lifted.

Jimmy knew. Not just about Jaime, but about all of it—the fear, the stakes, what it might cost him. And instead of backing away, his little brother had stepped up.

You're my brother. That's not gonna change because Mom's got a stick up her ass about church stuff.

Alex laughed—a wet, shaky sound—and wiped his face with his shirt.

He thought about Jimmy back in Oxford, in his room with his angry music, feeling invisible in a house where Alex had always felt like a stranger. Two brothers who'd spent years circling each other, never knowing they were both drowning in different ways.

Maybe it wasn't too late to change that.

LATER THAT NIGHT, Alex told Jaime everything.

They were in Jaime's room, Alex's head in his lap, Jaime's fingers running absently through his hair. When Alex finished talking, Jaime was quiet for a long moment.

"So he cried," Jaime said finally. "When you told him what you were afraid of."

"No. I cried." Alex closed his eyes. "He just... listened. And then he said he'd have my back. No matter what."

"Your fifteen-year-old brother said that?"

"With a lot more swearing. But yeah."

Jaime's hand stilled. "Alex. That's huge."

"I know." Alex opened his eyes, looked up at him. "I didn't expect it. Any of it. I thought he'd be weird about the gay thing, or pissed that I didn't tell him. But he just... got it. Once I explained what I was scared of, he got it."

"He sounds like a good kid."

"He is. Under all the bullshit." Alex smiled slightly. "He threatened to kick your ass, by the way."

"Noted. I'll be on my best behavior."

They were quiet for a moment. Jaime resumed stroking Alex's hair.

"This doesn't fix anything with my parents," Alex said. "I still don't know how to tell them. Or what they'll do."

"I know."

"But having Jimmy..." Alex trailed off, trying to find the words. "It's different now. Knowing someone in my family is on my side. Even if everything goes to shit."

"It's not nothing."

"No. It's not."

Jaime leaned down and kissed his forehead. "When you're ready. I'll be there. And apparently so will your foul-mouthed little brother."

Alex laughed. It came easier now. "God help us all."

They lay there in the quiet, tangled together, the weight of the day slowly settling into something Alex could carry.

His brother knew. And he was on his side.

PART III

RECKONING

14

Preparation

"Who are you texting?"

"No one. Just Alex."

"Alex." Mindy said it flat. "You've been texting him a lot lately."

"He's my friend."

"He's your friend from high school. You're at Duke now. You have new friends."

Brad didn't respond. He didn't know how to explain it—this pull he felt back toward Oxford, toward the people who knew him before all of this. Before he became Brad McPherson, Duke Basketball. Back when he was just Brad, the tall kid who was pretty good at sports and liked hanging out with his weird artsy friend.

"He's my friend," Brad said. "Is that a problem?"

"He's your friend from high school." Mindy closed her laptop. "You're at Duke now. You have new friends."

Brad didn't respond. He didn't know how to explain it—this pull he felt back toward Oxford, toward the people who knew him before all of this.

Mindy watched him for a long moment. Her eyes had gone sharp—that calculating look she got when she was figuring something out. Brad had seen it a hundred times, usually directed at other people. Never at him.

"What's going on with you?" she asked. "You've been weird for weeks. I'm trying to plan our future here, and you're texting some nobody from Ohio."

"He's not a nobody."

"You're at Duke. You're going to the NBA. Why are you so hung up on people who aren't going anywhere?"

"Don't talk about him like that."

Mindy's eyebrows rose. "Okay. Wow." She leaned back, arms crossed. "I've never seen you get this worked up about anyone. Including me."

"That's not fair."

"Isn't it?" She studied him for a moment, something shifting in her expression. "Wait. Is this about what I told you? At dinner that time?"

Brad stiffened.

"It is, isn't it? You're still hung up on the whole Alex-being-gay thing." She shook her head. "I told you—just be supportive if it ever comes up. Don't go fishing for some big confession. That's weird, Brad."

"What? No. I'm not—"

"What do you think is going to happen? He's going to pour his heart out and suddenly you're best friends again?" She shook her head. "I don't get you sometimes. Why are you being so weird about this?"

Brad looked down at his phone. Alex's last text stared back at him: *Good! Busy with classes. How's Duke?*

Surface level. Polite. The kind of response you'd give to someone you used to know.

Maybe Mindy was right. Maybe too much time had passed.

Maybe he and Alex were just... done. Limited to "how are things?" forever.

But that wasn't what he wanted. That wasn't why he kept texting.

The truth was, Brad wasn't trying to get Alex to come out. He wasn't fishing for confessions or trying to prove Mindy wrong. He was trying to clear his conscience. All those years he'd let the friendship drift—too busy with basketball, too wrapped up in Mindy's plans, too focused on becoming whoever everyone expected him to be. He'd let Alex slip away without even noticing.

And now, sitting in his dorm room at Duke with a future laid out in front of him like a highway he never asked to drive on, all he could think about was what he'd lost.

Alex had been his friend. His real friend. Not because Brad was popular or talented or dating the right girl. Just because they liked each other. Just because they fit.

When was the last time anyone had liked him just for being him?

"Brad." Mindy's voice cut through. "Are you even listening to me?"

"Yeah. Sorry."

"My parents are coming for the first game. And then we're all heading down to West Palm for Thanksgiving. Mom's already planning the dinner—she's got Dad's business partners coming, the Hendersons, the whole crowd. This is important, Brad. This is our future."

Brad nodded. He'd heard this before. The beach house. The connections. The dinners with people whose names he couldn't keep straight. Mindy's father sizing him up like an investment. Her mother already planning the wedding they hadn't discussed.

"I need you focused," Mindy continued. "Not moping around texting people from Ohio. Not being weird about your high school friend who's probably off doing... whatever gay guys do at art school."

"Mindy—"

"I'm serious." She stood up, smoothing her skirt. "You've got the season starting. You've got your future to think about. Scouts are going to be watching, Brad. This is everything we've been working toward."

We, Brad thought. *When did it become we?*

He remembered sophomore year, when Mindy had first attached herself to him. He'd been flattered—she was pretty, popular, the kind of girl who didn't usually look twice at guys like him. She'd seen potential in him, she'd said. A future she could help build. She'd push him. Make him into something.

And she had. Here he was at Duke, just like she'd planned.

So why did it feel like he'd lost something along the way?

THE BREAKING POINT came three nights later.

Mindy was on his bed, laptop open, scrolling through photos of table settings. "Mom thinks we should do the seafood tower again this year, but I told her that's so 2019. What do you think about a raw bar instead? More interactive."

Brad was at his desk, phone in hand, not listening.

> hey man just checking in hope you're doing okay here if you ever need anything.

He stared at the message before sending it. It sounded desperate. Needy. Like he was begging Alex to throw him a lifeline.

Maybe he was.

"Brad." Mindy's voice had an edge. "I asked you a question."

"Sorry. What?"

"Raw bar or seafood tower. For Thanksgiving."

"Whatever you think is best."

"That's not an answer." She sat up, closing her laptop with a sharp click. "Who are you texting?"

"No one."

"Let me see."

"Mindy—"

"Let me see your phone, Brad."

He handed it over. Watched her scroll through his messages with Alex—the awkward check-ins, the surface-level responses, the desperate reaching for something that wasn't there anymore.

"Jesus Christ." She tossed the phone back at him. "This is pathetic. You're texting him like you're in love with him or something."

"I'm not—"

"You know what? I don't even care." She stood up, gathering her things. "I've spent four years building this with you. Four years. And you're sitting here mooning over some guy from high school who doesn't even want to talk to you."

"That's not fair."

"My friends warned me, you know. Back when we started dating." Her voice was rising now. "They said you were just another Oxford boy. That you'd peak in high school and never amount to anything. But I told them they were wrong. I believed in you. I—"

She stopped.

Just stopped. Mid-sentence. Her mouth still open, hand frozen on her laptop bag.

Brad watched something shift behind her eyes. The anger drained out of her face, replaced by something worse. Something flat and final.

She didn't say another word. Just finished packing her bag, slipped on her jacket, and walked to the door.

"Where are you going?" Brad asked.

Nothing.

"Mindy. Come on. Where are you going?"

She didn't turn around. Didn't stop. Just opened the door and walked out.

Brad sat there in the silence, phone still in his hand.

She'll get over it, he told himself. *She's just pissed. We've had fights before.*

He thought about going after her, but decided against it. Better to give her space. Let her cool down. She'd text him later tonight, or maybe tomorrow morning. They'd talk it out. That's how it always worked.

He looked back at his phone. At Alex's name on the screen.

She'll be back, he thought. *It'll blow over.*

But she never came back.

TWO DAYS PASSED. No texts. No calls. Nothing.

On the third day, he drove to her apartment. She answered the door in yoga pants and a Duke sweatshirt, hair pulled back, no makeup. Her eyes were red. She'd been crying—really crying, not the performative kind she used when she wanted something.

"Took you long enough," she said.

"I was giving you space."

"Space." She laughed—ugly, bitter. "You weren't giving me space, Brad. You just didn't care enough to show up."

"That's not—"

"Three days. Three fucking days. And the only reason you're here now is because you finally ran out of excuses." She shook her head. "You're pathetic."

"Mindy—"

"No. You don't get to 'Mindy' me." Her voice cracked, but the anger held. "I've been sitting here like an idiot, waiting for you to prove me wrong. And you couldn't even do that."

Brad stood there. He had nothing.

"You know what the worst part is? I actually loved you. I actually thought we had something." She wiped her face, furious at the tears. "Four years. Four years of my life, and you were never even here. You were always somewhere else. Thinking about home. About Alex. About whatever bullshit mattered more than me."

"I didn't mean to—"

"You never mean to. That's the problem." She crossed her arms. "You're the same guy I met freshman year. I thought I could make you into something. But you're nothing, Brad. You're just... nothing."

The word landed like a slap.

"I'm done." She grabbed the door. "I'm a freshman at Duke. I've got options. And I'm not wasting another second on someone who can't even look me in the eye and tell me I'm wrong."

Brad couldn't. Because she wasn't.

"That's what I thought." She stepped back. "Lose my number."

The door slammed in his face.

Brad stood in the hallway, ears ringing, trying to remember how to breathe.

ALEX WAS in the library when his phone buzzed.

> BRAD - DUKE
>
> i fucked up
>
> mindy left me
>
> really fucked up

Alex stared at the screen. Their texts were usually just surface stuff—"how's it going," "good, you?"—and then nothing for weeks. This was different.

said im nothing

like actually said

to my face

shit sorry

i dont even

i dnt know

sorry

u ok?

no

sitting in my car in the parking lot

cant go back thre

everyones gnna know

fuck

sorry shldnt be txting you this

its fine what happened?

dnt know

she kept sayin im not there

like im never there

shes right im not

dnt even know where i am

does that make sense

prolly not

srry

Alex shifted in his seat. He didn't know what to do with this.

Brad was always the one who had it together. The plan. The future. The girl.

> dnt apolgize

keep thinkin bout when we were kids

you me jason

before

miss that

miss being tht

whoever that was

dnt know anymore

> me too

really?

u have your art thing

figured it out

i just have bsktball

dnnt even know if i like it

dont know if ever did

fuck

sorry ima mess

He wanted to help, but this wasn't Jason—where he'd already know the right words before Jason even finished the sentence. He and Brad hadn't talked—really talked—since they were kids. Maybe not even then.

> focus on basketball?

> thing at a time

yeah

yeah ok

srry for dumping

we dnt tlk anymore

not really

don't know why i txt you

its ok glad u did

u got ur own shit

should go

sorry again

The texts stopped. Alex stared at the screen, his stomach tight. Brad was unraveling—that much was clear. But Alex didn't know how to reach him. Didn't know if he even could. They'd been friends once, a long time ago. Now they were just two people who used to know each other.

The conversation trailed off. Alex set his phone down and stared at the wall.

"Everything okay?" Jaime was across the table, looking up from his notes.

"Brad and Mindy broke up."

"Oh." Jaime set his pen down. "Is he alright?"

"I don't know. He seems pretty lost." Alex picked up his phone, scrolled back through the messages. "I want to help, but I don't know how. We haven't really talked in years. Not about real stuff. And everything I said was just... I don't know. 'Give it time.' 'Focus on basketball.' Stuff that doesn't..."

"Sometimes that's all you can do."

"I know. I just..." Alex trailed off, staring at the phone. "I don't know. It's weird. He was a big part of my life back then. And now we're just... nothing. I guess."

Jaime was quiet for a moment. "You moved on. That happens."

"Yeah." Alex set the phone down. "I just feel like I should be doing more. Or feeling more. Something."

"Maybe there's nothing more to do."

Alex didn't respond. He knew Jaime was probably right. But there was still something underneath—a guilt he couldn't quite name.

THE WEEK CREPT FORWARD. November settled over campus in gray skies and dead leaves. Most colleges held Parent's Weekend in October, tied to homecoming and football. But Oakwood had no football team—one of the things Alex had liked about it—so they'd scheduled theirs for mid-November instead. A chance for parents to check in before Thanksgiving break. An opportunity for families to reconnect.

Jaime's parents were flying in Thursday evening. Alex's parents would arrive Friday just before the banquet dinner that night.

They still hadn't figured out what to do.

"We could just be careful," Alex said. They were in Jaime's room, sprawled across his bed in the fading light. "Not say anything. Get through the weekend and deal with it later."

Jaime was quiet for a moment. Then: "You know what? I think you're overthinking this."

Alex looked over at him. "What do you mean?"

"I mean—" Jaime sat up, facing him. "Look, I know I have it easy. My parents already know I'm gay. They already know about you. And honestly? I'm excited for them to meet you. Like, actually excited. My dad keeps saying he wants to take us to dinner. Us. His son and his son's boyfriend. I never imagined my dad saying something like that."

Alex didn't respond.

"And yeah, I get how scary this feels for you. I'm not discounting that. But there's good stuff too, Alex. You're going to love my mom. Seriously. And my dad is going to embarrass me with stories about when I was a kid, and it's going to be great." Jaime paused. "And yes, we can hide. If that's what you need to do with your parents. We'll be careful. And if they freak out anyway... I don't know. That's bad. I won't pretend to know how to feel about that."

"Jaime—"

"But it's not all shit, you know?" Jaime's voice had an edge now. "You've got me. You've got my parents, who already want to meet you. Jimmy knows. Jason knows. Jenn knows. You've got all these people in your corner, and you treat every single one of them knowing like it's some kind of problem."

Alex blinked. "I don't—"

"You do though. And honestly?" Jaime looked away for a second, then back. "It kind of pisses me off."

Alex stared at him. He'd never seen Jaime upset. Not once. Jaime was the one who calmed everyone down, who smoothed things over, who always knew the right thing to say. He didn't get mad. He didn't push.

But right now, Jaime looked upset. At him.

"Listen, babe." Jaime's voice softened, but only a little. "I get it. Well—I do and I don't. I'm lucky. I know that. But the more you let your parents get in your head, the more you push me out. And everyone else who loves you."

Silence.

Alex hadn't thought about it that way. He knew Jaime was right. But he was afraid.

"I can guess," Jaime continued, "but why? What are you actually afraid of? What happens if they find out? They'll kick you out? Hurt you? What?"

Alex opened his mouth. Closed it. He'd asked himself these questions before, but he always stopped. It was like walking toward a cliff in the middle of the night—knowing something terrible was out there, even if you couldn't see it.

"I don't..." He tried again. "They'd kick me out. I'd be home-less. I'd have nowhere to go."

But even as he said it, his mind pushed back. That wasn't true. He had places. Jason's mom had already told him he was welcome. Jaime's parents would take him in. People wouldn't let him live on the streets.

"They'd hurt me," he tried.

But that wasn't true either. His dad had never laid a hand on him. His mom had spanked them as kids, but nothing serious. He couldn't actually imagine either of them physically hurting him.

So what was it? What was the big scary thing he couldn't look at?

Jaime was watching him. Not angry anymore—just worried. Waiting.

Alex felt something cracking open in his chest. The fear he'd been circling for months, maybe years, finally taking shape.

"I'm scared they won't love me anymore."

That was it. That was all of it. The words came out small and broken, and there was nothing else to say.

Jaime's face changed. The frustration was gone. Something in his eyes shifted—a recognition, maybe, of what Alex had just placed in his hands. This wasn't just worry about a weekend. This was the deepest part of him. The thing he'd never said out loud, never let himself fully feel.

And he'd given it to Jaime.

"I'm sorry," Jaime said quietly. "I didn't mean to push. I just—I want us to be happy. I want you to stop hurting so much."

Alex wiped his face with the back of his hand. "Can you just hold me? Please?"

Jaime pulled him close without another word. Alex buried his face in Jaime's chest, feeling small and scared and strangely lighter. Like something that had been locked inside him for years had finally been let out.

Jaime didn't say anything. He was eighteen years old, same as Alex. He didn't have answers. He didn't know how to fix this.

So he just held him.

Outside, the last light faded from the sky. Parent's Weekend was three days away.

15

The Proposal

Susan Stamford hugged like she was trying to squeeze the life out of you and put it back in better than before.

Alex learned this approximately three seconds after meeting her.

"And you must be Alex!" She had him wrapped up before he could even extend his hand, pulling him in tight enough that his feet nearly left the ground. She smelled like expensive perfume and airplane and something warm underneath. "Oh, Jaime, he's adorable. Look at him!"

"Mom, you're crushing him."

"I am not. I'm welcoming him." She pulled back just enough to look at Alex's face, her hands still on his shoulders. "You're family now. This is what we do."

Behind her, a tall man with kind eyes and graying hair was already embracing Jaime. When he looked over at Alex, there was something instantly calming about him—a stillness that balanced his wife's energy perfectly.

"I'm Thom," he said, releasing Jaime and extending his hand. "But you probably guessed that."

"Uh, hi. Mr. Stam—"

"Thom. Just Thom." His handshake was warm, unhurried. "We've heard a lot about you."

"All good things," Susan added, remaining close. "Well, mostly. Jaime did mention you have questionable taste in coffee."

"Mom."

"What? I'm just saying. We'll work on it." She looped her arm through Alex's like they'd known each other for years and started walking toward baggage claim. "Now, tell me everything. How did you two meet? Jaime's been so stingy with details."

Alex looked back at Jaime helplessly. Jaime just shrugged and smiled—*welcome to my world.*

THEY'D ARRIVED A DAY EARLY. Something about limited flight options from LaGuardia, Susan explained, but really they'd wanted the extra time. Thom admitted as much over the rental car paperwork.

"We haven't seen him since August," he said quietly to Alex while Susan interrogated Jaime about his classes. "And now there's you. We wanted to actually meet you, not just shake hands at some formal dinner."

"I appreciate that. Sir. Thom." Alex caught himself. "Sorry."

"Don't apologize. And don't be nervous." Thom signed the last form and slid it across the counter. "Susan's a lot, I know. But she means well. She's just excited."

"About what?"

Thom looked at him with something like amusement. "About you. About Jaime having someone. About all of it." He pocketed the keys. "You're the first person he's ever brought home. Well—brought to us. You know what I mean."

Alex hadn't thought about it that way. He was Jaime's first. First boyfriend. First introduction to the parents. First everything.

The weight of that settled somewhere in his chest.

THEY WANTED TO SEE EVERYTHING.

The dorm ("It's so small! How do you both fit?" "Mom, we have separate rooms." "Oh, sure you do."). The dining hall ("This is what they feed you? Thom, we're sending care packages."). The quad where Alex and Jaime had first talked. The art building where Alex spent most of his time.

Susan asked questions constantly. About his classes, his drawings, his hometown, his brothers. Thom listened more than he spoke, but when he did, it was always something that made Alex feel seen.

"Jaime says you're talented," Thom said while they walked across campus. "But he also says you don't believe it."

Alex felt his face warm. "I'm okay. There's a lot of people better than me."

"There always will be. Doesn't mean you're not good." Thom smiled slightly. "I was a dancer, back in the day. Spent half my career convinced I wasn't good enough. Wasted a lot of years on that."

"What changed?"

"I got older. Realized that 'good enough' was a moving target I'd never hit. So I stopped chasing it and just danced." He shrugged. "You might try that with your art."

Alex didn't know what to say. No one had ever talked to him like that—like his doubt was normal, manageable, something he could outgrow.

"Thanks," he managed.

"Don't mention it." Thom clapped him on the shoulder. "Now come on. Susan's probably already planning your wedding."

Alex's heart skipped. "What?"

"I'm kidding." Thom laughed. "Mostly."

. . .

SOMEWHERE BETWEEN THE campus tour and dinner, Susan pulled Jaime aside.

Alex saw them across the quad—Susan's hand on Jaime's arm, her head tilted in that way parents do when they're asking something important. Jaime glanced back at Alex, then said something to his mother that made her expression shift.

When they rejoined the group, Susan looked at Alex differently. Not with pity—nothing that obvious. But with a softness that hadn't been there before. Like she understood something now that she hadn't earlier.

She linked her arm through his again as they walked to dinner.

"You know," she said quietly, "whatever happens this weekend —with your parents, with any of it—you have a place with us. Always."

Alex's throat tightened. "Jaime told you."

"He told me you're scared. That's all I needed to know." She squeezed his arm. "You're not alone, Alex. I know it might feel that way sometimes. But you're not."

He didn't trust himself to speak. Just nodded.

Susan patted his arm and shifted back to her bright, over-whelming self. "Now! Jaime mentioned there's an Italian place? I'm starving, and I refuse to eat another airport pretzel."

THE RESTAURANT WAS small and dim, tucked into a corner of town they'd never explored. An old man in a worn black suit seated them in a curved booth at the back, and Thom surprised everyone by ordering in Italian.

"Saremmo onorati se scegliessi il nostro pasto, per favore," he said, stumbling slightly over the words.

The old man's face lit up. He clapped his hands together and disappeared into the kitchen.

"Show off," Susan muttered, but she was smiling.

"Where did you learn Italian?" Alex asked.

"I danced in Europe for years. Picked up a few things." Thom reached for the bread basket. "Mostly how to order food and ask where the bathroom is."

"The essentials," Jaime added.

"Exactly."

The food came in waves—bruschetta, then pasta, then something with veal that Alex couldn't pronounce but couldn't stop eating. The waiter returned with a bottle of wine. Thom swirled it, sniffed, nodded approval, and the waiter began pouring.

Alex watched the dark red liquid fill his glass. He'd never had wine before. Never had anything alcoholic, really—his parents weren't drinkers, and Oxford wasn't exactly the kind of place where kids snuck into bars.

Jaime reached for his glass easily, then caught Alex's hesitation. He glanced at his dad.

Thom noticed too. "First time with wine?"

"That obvious?"

"Nothing wrong with that." Thom slid his own glass closer. "Here—smell it first. You're looking for fruit, maybe a little oak. This one's a Chianti, so it'll have some cherry, maybe plum."

Alex leaned in, feeling slightly ridiculous, but Thom's manner was so unhurried that it didn't feel like a test. Just a lesson.

"Now take a small sip. Let it sit on your tongue for a second before you swallow."

Alex tried. It was... okay. Not bad. Not great. A little bitter, a little warm going down.

"What do you think?" Susan asked.

"I think I need more practice."

Thom smiled. "That's the right answer."

Alex took another sip. It was growing on him. Maybe.

"Just go easy," Susan said, refilling her own glass. "I don't need my son-in-law drunk on our first dinner together."

"Mom!" Jaime groaned.

She shrugged, grinning. "What? I'm just being practical."

SUSAN TOLD stories about Jaime as a kid. Thom told stories about Susan. Jaime protested loudly and ineffectively while Alex laughed harder than he had in weeks.

"He used to make us watch The Little Mermaid every single night," Susan said, dabbing her eyes. "Every. Single. Night. For a year."

"Mom!"

"What? It's adorable. You wanted to be Ariel."

"I wanted to be *Flounder*."

"That's worse!"

Alex was crying with laughter. Actual tears. He couldn't remember the last time he'd laughed like this—openly, without holding anything back.

"See?" Jaime said, gesturing at his parents. "See what I grew up with?"

"They're amazing," Alex said. And meant it.

Jaime's face softened. "Yeah. They are."

THE TEASING CONTINUED THROUGH DESSERT.

"So," Susan said, swirling her wine, "when are you two going to adopt and give me grandchildren?"

"Mom!"

"What? I'm just asking. I didn't even know I wanted grand-children until I met Alex. Now I'm picturing little curly-haired artists running around."

"We've been dating for two months."

"And? Your father proposed to me after three weeks."

"That's different."

"How?"

"You were both insane."

"We were in love," Susan corrected. "Same thing, really."

Thom raised his glass. "She's not wrong."

Alex watched the exchange, something warm spreading through his chest. He liked this.

"Oh! I just thought of something." Susan sat up straighter, her eyes brightening. "If you two ever do get married—and I'm not saying when, just if—there's this venue in the Catskills that would be absolutely perfect. Glass walls, mountain views, seats about two hundred—"

"Mom. We're eating dessert."

"I'm just brainstorming! It doesn't hurt to plan ahead."

Jaime's face had gone red. He turned to Alex, mortified. "I'm so sorry. She does this. I should have warned you."

"Warned him about what?" Susan looked genuinely confused. "I'm being helpful."

"You're being insane."

"I'm being a mother." She waved her spoon at him. "There's a difference. Barely."

Thom leaned over toward Alex. "Get used to it," he murmured. "I did. About twenty years ago."

"I heard that," Susan said.

"You were meant to."

Alex laughed—and then, before he could stop himself: "Does she also plan the honeymoon, or do we get some say in that?"

The table went quiet for half a second. Then Susan burst out laughing—a real laugh, surprised and delighted.

"Oh, I like him." She pointed her spoon at Jaime. "Don't mess this up."

"Thanks for the vote of confidence, Mom."

But Jaime was grinning, and so was Alex. He wasn't just watching anymore. He was part of this.

. . .

THE DRIVE back to campus was more of the same—Susan asking about their plans, Thom making dry observations, Jaime rolling his eyes while secretly loving every minute.

"So when's the wedding?" Susan asked, not for the first time.

"Mom. Seriously."

"I'm just saying, you should lock this one down. He's cute, he's talented, he laughs at your father's jokes—"

"Everyone laughs at my jokes," Thom interjected.

"—and he clearly adores you. What more do you need?"

Jaime groaned. "Can we please talk about literally anything else?"

"Fine, fine." Susan held up her hands in surrender. "I'll stop. For now."

The car quieted for a few minutes. Alex leaned against Jaime's shoulder, watching the streetlights pass.

"Alex, did Jaime ever tell you I plan weddings for a living?" Susan asked, turning slightly in her seat. "That Catskills venue I mentioned at dinner? I wasn't kidding. I could make a few calls—"

"Mom!"

"What? I'm just making conversation."

"You're planning our wedding again."

"I am not. I'm simply mentioning that I have resources, should anyone ever need them." She sniffed. "Whenever that might be."

"You know what," Jaime said, "maybe we should just get it over with. Get engaged. Shut her up."

Everyone laughed.

"I'm serious," Jaime continued, playing it up. "It's the only way. She'll never stop otherwise."

"He's not wrong," Thom said from the driver's seat.

"See? Even Dad agrees."

Susan laughed. "Fine, fine. I'll stop. For now."

The car quieted. Alex was still smiling, shaking his head at the absurdity of it all, when he realized Jaime had gone quiet beside him.

He glanced over.

Jaime was looking at him. Not laughing anymore. Something in his expression had shifted—the teasing gone, replaced by something else entirely.

"Would you want to?"

Alex's laugh caught in his throat. "What?"

"Get engaged." Jaime's voice was quieter now. "Would you want to?"

The car went silent.

Alex stared at him. "You're joking."

"I'm not."

"Jaime—" Alex sat up straighter. "We've known each other since September. We're freshmen. We have—I don't know—three-plus years of college ahead of us, and then jobs, and who knows what else. We're eighteen. We don't even know what we're doing next semester, let alone—"

"I know."

"—and getting engaged is a huge thing. A real thing. People plan for that. They wait until they're sure, until they've been together for years, until—"

"Alex."

"—it's just, we're so young, and there's so much that could happen, and I'm not saying I don't love you, because I do, I really do, but—"

"Alex."

He stopped. Looked at Jaime.

"I'm not suggesting we get married tomorrow," Jaime said calmly. "I'm just calling it what it is. At least in my mind." He paused. "I want to have that commitment to you. I feel like I already do. I know I do."

In the front seat, Susan's breath had gone still. Thom's hands tightened on the steering wheel.

"You're serious?" Alex asked.

"As I've ever been."

Alex felt something shift inside him. All those rational arguments—they were still there, still valid. They were eighteen. They were kids. There was so much they didn't know.

But looking at Jaime—at his steady eyes, his certain expression, the quiet confidence that had drawn Alex to him from the very first day—the whole thing was preposterous, but none of that seemed to matter.

"Okay," Alex said.

"Okay, then." Jaime nodded once, like they'd just settled on where to get lunch tomorrow.

They both turned back toward the window. The streetlights passed. The car hummed along.

Silence.

Susan waited. For the hug, the kiss, the celebration. Something.

Finally, she couldn't take it anymore.

"Okay? That's it? *Okay?*" She twisted around in her seat. "What the hell is wrong with you two?"

Jaime and Alex burst out laughing. They'd almost forgotten his parents were there, listening to every word.

"What—what just happened?" Thom asked, bewildered.

Susan was already answering: "I think we really do have a son-in-law now. Although 'okay' didn't seem very final to me."

Alex was still laughing, but there were tears in his eyes now—the good kind. He turned to Jaime and made a show of it, playing it up for Susan's benefit.

"Yes, Jaime," he said formally. "Yes, I'll marry you."

And he leaned in and kissed him.

Susan let out a proper yelp. "Oh, my baby!"

"Mom!"

"What? How often do I get to witness these things? Give me a break!" She was practically bouncing in her seat. "I would give you both the biggest hug right now, but we're driving."

Thom was grinning, shaking his head. "No weddings until after graduation."

"Okay, Dad," Jaime laughed.

"Got that, son?"

"I already said okay," Jaime rolled his eyes, still smiling.

"Not you." Thom glanced in the rearview mirror. "Alex."

Alex paused.

Son.

He looked at Jaime, who just shrugged—this wasn't part of any plan. That was just... Dad.

Alex bit his lip, holding back something that threatened to spill over. The word he'd been so afraid of losing. The belonging he'd been terrified he'd never have.

And here it was. Offered freely. Without conditions.

In the passenger seat, Susan made a small sound—something between a gasp and a laugh—and pressed her hand to her chest.

Jaime squeezed Alex's hand, hard. When Alex glanced over, Jaime's eyes were wet.

None of them said anything else. They didn't need to.

Thom was still grinning as he turned into the dorm parking lot.

Alex had a family.

A real one. One that chose him.

Tomorrow, his parents would arrive. Tomorrow, everything might fall apart.

But tonight, he was home.

16

Found

Alex didn't notice the texts until Thom was pulling into the parking lot.

His phone had been on silent during dinner, and then—well, then Jaime had proposed in the back seat of a rental car, and checking messages hadn't exactly been a priority. But now, as the car slowed to a stop, he glanced down and saw the notifications stacked on his screen.

Six messages. All from Brad.

"Everything okay?" Jaime asked.

Alex didn't answer. He was reading.

> **BRAD - DUKE**
>
> hey man
>
> know this is crazy but I'm driving up
>
> been on road all day
>
> didn't know where to go on campus so siri taking me to the student center lot
>
> about 2 hrs out

gonna surprise you.

That was sent almost two hours ago. Brad had already been driving for hours before he even texted.

here

hope you're not mad. I know I should've called before I left Duke but I just got in my car and started driving.

An hour and a half ago.

sorry

this was stupid

An hour ago.

ur prob busy

gonna wait

txt me

Forty minutes ago.

i fucked up

gonna head out

maybe drive home n crash at my folk

sorry 2 cos any prob

Twenty minutes ago.

leaving

sorry

Five minutes ago.

"Alex?" Jaime leaned over, reading the screen. "Is that Brad?"

"He drove here. From Duke." Alex's voice sounded strange to his own ears. "He's been waiting in the student center lot for almost two hours."

"What's going on, boys?" Susan turned in her seat.

"One of Alex's friends from high school," Jaime said. "He's going through a tough time. Texted last week—broke up with his girlfriend. Sounds like he drove up here to see Alex."

"He's still close by," Alex said, already pulling up Brad's number. "That last text was five minutes ago. He can't have gotten far."

He hit call.

Brad picked up on the second ring. "Alex? Shit, I'm sorry, I didn't mean to—"

"Where are you?"

"I just pulled out of the parking lot. I'm on—I don't know, some road with a gas station. I'm sorry, I shouldn't have just shown up like this. I don't know what I was thinking."

"Turn around."

Silence.

"Brad. Turn around and come to Harrison Hall. The freshman dorms. I'll text you the address."

"I don't want to mess up your night. You're probably with—"

"Brad." Alex's voice was firm. "Turn around."

A long pause. Then, quietly: "Okay."

THE CAR PULLED into the lot three minutes later.

Alex recognized Brad's old Honda before he could make out the figure behind the wheel. It had been Brad's since junior year —a hand-me-down from his older cousin, perpetually in need of an oil change.

He stepped out of the Stamfords' rental, Jaime beside him. Susan and Thom followed, standing by the car, watching.

Brad climbed out slowly. He was wearing a Duke hoodie, the hood pulled up despite being inside all day. Even in the dim parking lot light, Alex could see he looked rough—unshaved, tired, smaller somehow than he remembered.

"Alex, I'm so sorry," Brad started, eyes darting to the unfamiliar faces behind him. "I didn't mean to crash your—I don't even know what I'm doing here. This was stupid. I should go."

"Brad—"

"No, seriously. You've got people here, and I just showed up like some kind of—" He stopped, noticing Susan approaching. His shoulders tensed.

"You must be Brad." Susan's voice was warm, unhurried. She extended her hand like they were meeting at a dinner party. "I'm Susan. Jaime's mother."

Brad shook her hand, visibly confused. "Uh, hi. I'm sorry, I didn't mean to interrupt—"

"Have you eaten?"

"What?"

"Have you eaten anything? You drove from Duke, yes? That's —six hours? More?"

"About six, yeah. I didn't stop."

Susan turned to Thom, who was already nodding. "There's that diner Jaime mentioned. The one with the pie."

"I couldn't—" Brad started.

"Nonsense." Susan was already guiding him toward the rental car, her hand on his arm in that way she had—firm but gentle, like she'd done this a thousand times. "You drove six hours. You're getting something warm in you before anything else."

Brad looked back at Alex helplessly.

"Just go with it," Alex said. "Trust me."

THE DINER WAS MOSTLY empty at this hour—a few truckers at the counter, an elderly couple in a booth by the window. They slid into a corner table, Brad ending up between Alex and Jaime, with Susan and Thom across.

A waitress appeared. Susan ordered coffee for the table and insisted Brad get whatever he wanted. He stared at the menu like it was written in another language.

"The turkey melt is good," Jaime offered. "If you're not sure."

"Okay. Yeah. That's fine."

The waitress left and silence settled over the table.

Brad stared at his hands. "I don't know why I drove here. I just—I was sitting in my room, and Mindy's gone, and everyone at Duke is..." He shook his head. "I didn't know where else to go."

"What about your parents?" Susan asked gently.

"They'd just tell me to focus on basketball. That's all they care about. That's all anyone cares about." He laughed—a hollow sound. "Brad McPherson, future NBA star. That's who I'm supposed to be. That's the plan."

"Whose plan?" Thom asked.

Brad looked up. "What?"

"Whose plan is it? Yours? Your parents'? Your girlfriend's?"

The question hung in the air. Brad opened his mouth, closed it.

"I was a dancer," Thom said. "Classical ballet. Started when I was six, went professional at nineteen. Everyone had plans for me—my instructors, my company, the critics. 'Thom Stamford, future principal dancer.' They mapped out my whole life."

Brad was listening now, really listening.

"And I was good. Good enough that I could've done it—the international tours, the starring roles, all of it. But somewhere along the way, I realized I was doing it for them. Not for me." Thom shrugged. "I loved dancing. I didn't love being a dancer. There's a difference."

"So what did you do?"

"I stopped. Opened a studio. Taught kids who actually wanted to be there." He smiled slightly. "Best decision I ever made. But it took me a long time to figure out that the plan everyone had for me wasn't my plan."

The food arrived. Brad stared at his sandwich like he'd forgotten how eating worked.

"What do you actually want, Brad?" Susan asked. "Not what everyone expects. What do you want?"

"I don't know." His voice cracked. "I used to just like playing ball. That's it. Just playing. With my friends, in the driveway, wherever. And then suddenly it became this whole thing—scholarships and scouts and Mindy planning our future, and I just..." He pressed the heels of his hands into his eyes. "I don't know who I am without all that. That's the fucked up part." He glanced at Susan and Thom. "Sorry. I didn't mean to—"

Thom waved him off. "You're fine."

"Take away the basketball star," Brad continued, "and I'm just... nobody."

"That's not true," Alex said quietly.

Brad looked at him.

"You're not nobody. You're my friend. You were my friend before any of this—before Duke, before Mindy, before any of it. Remember? We used to just hang out. Watch movies. Talk about stupid shit."

"That was a long time ago."

"So? Doesn't mean it wasn't real." Alex leaned forward. "Look, I don't know what you should do about Duke or basketball or any of that. But I know you don't have to be who everyone else expects. You can come back to Ohio if you want. Or stay at Duke. Or do something completely different. It doesn't matter. Just—be honest about what you actually want. And stop being afraid of what everyone else thinks."

Jaime caught Alex's eye. There was something in his expression—a raised eyebrow, a small smile. *You hearing yourself, babe?* Alex felt his own words land differently, realizing he was saying to Brad what he'd needed to hear himself.

"Since when did you get so wise?" Brad asked, a ghost of a smile crossing his face.

"I've always been wise. You just weren't listening."

"Bullshit." But a smirk was just starting to appear. "I was always listening. You just never talked."

"Fair point."

Brad picked up his sandwich, took a bite. Chewed slowly. Something in his shoulders relaxed—not all the way, but enough.

"I'm sorry," he said after a moment. "I'm a shitty friend. I got so wrapped up in Mindy and her bullshit—all those people who only gave a damn about me because I could play ball—and I just left you behind. You and Jason. I knew I was doing it and I did it anyway."

Alex was quiet for a moment. He couldn't deny it—he had felt abandoned. All those years of watching Brad drift further into a world Alex couldn't follow, wouldn't have wanted to follow even if he could.

"Yeah," Alex said finally. "You did."

Brad flinched.

"But we were kids. We were figuring shit out. And holding onto that doesn't help either of us." Alex shrugged. "We all get do-overs, right? So... let's just start again."

"Start again?" He scoffed.

"Yeah." Alex straightened up, extended his hand formally. "Hi. I'm Alex Robertson. Nice to meet you."

Brad stared at him. Then, slowly, he took his hand. "Brad McPherson."

"Good to meet you, Brad." Alex grinned. "And this is my fiancé, Jaime."

Brad nodded absently, still caught up in everything—the apology, the do-over, all of it. Then the word landed.

"Wait." He looked up. "Your what?"

Alex watched him process it. The confusion. The slow dawning. Brad opened his mouth, closed it. Opened it again. Nothing came out.

He didn't know what to say. Alex could see it—Brad's brain trying to catch up, trying to figure out how to respond, what the right thing was. The silence stretched.

Alex turned in the booth to face him directly. "Brad. I'm gay."

The words came out easier than he expected. Easier than they ever had. He'd said them to Jason, to Jimmy. But this was Brad—his oldest friend, the one he'd been most afraid to lose.

And it was easy.

Brad stared at him. Then, unexpectedly, he laughed. Just a small one, almost to himself.

"What's funny?" Alex asked.

"Nothing. It's just—" Brad shook his head. "Mindy told me. Back when we had dinner. She said everyone knew. Back in high school. Said I was the only one who didn't see it."

Alex felt the old sting, but it faded fast. "Yeah. I figured people talked."

"I'm sorry. I didn't—"

"No offense to your girlfriend," Alex cut in, then paused. "Wait, you said you broke up."

"Yeah."

"Then you mind if I say fuck her? And her friends?" Alex's voice was harder than Brad had ever heard it. "All those years of whispering behind my back. Fuck them."

Jaime flinched slightly—not at the words, but at the edge in Alex's voice. He caught his parents' eyes, gave them a small look. *It's okay. I'll explain later.*

Brad was quiet. Something shifted in his expression as he realized what had just happened. Alex had trusted him. Told him directly. After everything—after Brad had disappeared into Mindy's world, after years of barely talking—Alex had looked him in the eye and said it.

He reached over awkwardly, pulling Alex into a hug. It was

clumsy—they were wedged into a booth, and Brad's arms didn't quite know where to go. Alex stiffened for a second, unsure what was happening, then relaxed and hugged him back.

"I'm sorry," Brad said into his shoulder. "For being so fucking clueless. For all of it. And... thanks. For trusting me."

He pulled back, wiping his eyes quickly, then turned and reached toward Jaime. "And, uh, congratulations. To you. Both of you."

It was awkward—Brad half-standing in the booth, arm extended, not quite sure if he should hug Jaime or shake his hand. Jaime managed, pulling him into a brief, back-slapping embrace.

"Thanks, man."

Susan watched the whole exchange, then cleared her throat. "I think we could all use some pie. And coffee." She flagged down the waitress. "Whatever's best. Five slices. And refills all around."

The waitress nodded and disappeared.

"A toast," Susan announced, raising her coffee mug.

Jaime raised an eyebrow. "Over coffee?"

Susan didn't miss a beat. "We're in Ohio. What else do you want me to do?"

That broke it. Everyone laughed—real laughter, the tension finally releasing. Brad's shoulders dropped. Alex leaned back against the booth. Even Thom cracked a genuine smile.

"To new beginnings," Susan said, lifting her mug higher.

They clinked their cups together. It wasn't champagne. It wasn't fancy. But it was enough.

"So," Thom said after a moment, setting down his mug, "where are you staying tonight?"

Brad froze. "I... didn't think that far ahead."

"Of course you didn't." Thom looked at Alex. "I assume you have a room?"

"Yeah." Alex glanced at Jaime. "Brad can take mine. I'll stay with Jaime."

"Problem solved." Thom nodded once, like it was settled.

"I can't just—" Brad started.

"You can," Alex said. "And you will. We'll figure out the rest tomorrow."

"Thanks," Brad said. It was all he could manage.

"Wait till you see how tiny his room is," Jaime said. "You might end up sleeping in the hallway."

"It's not that small."

"Babe, I've seen closets bigger than your room."

Susan laughed. "Oh, you should have seen my dorm room back in the day. I swear it was smaller than our bathroom now. And I had a roommate. We had to coordinate just to open our dresser drawers—"

She launched into the story, Thom adding commentary, Jaime interjecting with jokes. Brad listened, not really following, just... watching. These people. This family that had folded him in without question.

He caught Alex smiling at Jaime—that soft, carefree look. In love. Actually in love.

Brad didn't know what to think. Didn't know what came next, or where he'd be tomorrow, or any of it.

But he was glad Alex had told him. That much, he knew.

17

The Silent Plea

The Robertson kitchen smelled like meatloaf.

It was Thursday night—the night before Parent's Weekend—and Elizabeth had made Bill's favorite. Scotty was pushing peas around his plate, Jimmy was eating in silence, and Bill was cutting his meat into precise squares, the way he always did.

"So," Bill said, not looking up from his plate, "just wanted to let you know—Mrs. Patterson will be here around two-thirty tomorrow. Your mother and I should be back by ten or so."

Jimmy's fork stopped halfway to his mouth. "Mrs. Patterson?"

"To watch you and Scotty while we're gone."

"You're kidding."

Bill glanced up. "It's just for a few hours."

"I'm fifteen. I don't need a babysitter."

"It's not up for discussion."

"Why not?" Jimmy set his fork down. "I can handle watching Scotty for one night. I do it all the time when you guys go out."

"That's different."

"How is it different?"

Bill's jaw tightened. "Because I said so."

"That's not a reason."

"James." Bill's voice carried a warning. "Drop it."

"No." Jimmy heard himself say it before he could stop. "I'm not dropping it. You're *just* driving two hours! It's not like you're flying to Egypt. I can handle—"

"James, I don't trust—" Bill stopped himself. But the damage was done.

Jimmy stared at him. The unfinished word hung in the air between them.

I don't trust you.

That's what he was going to say. That's what he'd been thinking this whole time. Not "it's different" or "because I said so." The real reason. The thing he almost let slip.

"Wow." Jimmy's voice came out strange. Hollow. "Good to know."

"That's not what I meant."

"Then what did you mean?"

Bill didn't answer.

"Why? You're driving two hours to see your real son. The one you actually give a shit about."

"Jimmy!" Elizabeth's voice cut in. "That's enough."

"No, it's not enough! I do everything right—sports, grades, everything—and you still treat me like I'm gonna burn the house down. Meanwhile, Alex gets to be your golden boy just because he went to some art school—"

"That's not fair," Bill said, his voice low. Dangerous.

"Not *fair*?" Jimmy laughed, harsh and bitter. "You took a whole day off work to drive him to that campus visit. You've never come to a single one of my track meets. Not one."

"That's different."

"How is it different?"

"Because—" Bill's hand came down on the table. Scotty flinched. "Because I said so."

"Oh, great. Because you said so. That's perfect, Dad. That's exactly the kind of—"

"James Robertson, you will lower your voice in my house."

"Or what?" Jimmy stood up, his chair scraping back. Something had cracked inside him. All the resentment he'd been swallowing for months—years, maybe—was flooding up his throat.

Bill rose slowly. His hand came up—

Jimmy stumbled backward, his legs catching against the chair, nearly toppling it.

"Bill!" Elizabeth's voice cut through like the slap she was sure was intended for her son.

Bill froze. He looked at his own raised hand like he didn't recognize it. Like he hadn't known what he was doing. The rage drained from his face, replaced by something confused. Horrified.

Scotty's fork clattered to his plate. His lower lip trembled, and then he was crying—small, hiccuping sobs that filled the silence.

Bill lowered his hand slowly. His voice came out rough, shaken. "Sit. Down."

But the damage was done. Jimmy had seen it. They all had.

"No." Jimmy's voice was shaking now, but he couldn't stop. "You want to know the real difference between me and Alex? I'm *here*. I'm the one who actually sticks around. I'm the one who does everything you ask. And you still don't see me."

"James—"

"I get good grades. I practice—every single day, Dad, every day—I do my chores, I don't complain, I don't—" His voice cracked. "I haven't even had a girlfriend because I'm too busy trying to be—trying to be what you want, and it's never—" He was talking too fast now, words piling up. "And none of it matters! Because Alex—perfect fucking Alex—he never had to try at anything. He just draws his little pictures and everyone thinks he's so special. And you—you're driving two hours to see him, and

I bet he's not even—he's probably just—off at parties with his perfect fucking boyfriend while you think he's—"

Jimmy stopped.

The word hung in the air.

Boyfriend.

He felt it land before anyone reacted. Felt the weight of it, the wrongness, the oh-God-no of what he'd just said.

"Wait—no." His voice came out too high. "I didn't—that's not —" He looked at his mother's face. His father's. Made it worse. "I didn't mean that. I was just angry. I meant friend. His friend. That's what I—" He was drowning. Every word dug the hole deeper. "It came out wrong. I was just—I didn't—"

He couldn't breathe. Couldn't think. His mouth kept moving but nothing he said was helping. Nothing was going to help.

Please. Please. Please let them believe me.

Silence.

Elizabeth's fork clattered against her plate. Bill had gone very still.

"What did you say?" Bill's voice was quiet. Too quiet.

Jimmy's heart was pounding. He could feel the blood draining from his face. He wanted to try again—to deny it, take it back, make them unhear it—but his father was looking at him with that same coldness from before. The same look he'd had right before his hand came up.

"His... boyfriend?" Bill stepped closer, and Jimmy flinched. "What are you talking about?"

Jimmy's mouth opened. Closed. No words came.

"James." Bill's voice was harder now. "What boyfriend?"

And Jimmy—stupid, angry, terrified Jimmy—looked at his father's face and knew there was no way out. The lie had already failed. They'd seen through it. And now Bill was standing over him, waiting, and Jimmy was fifteen years old and exhausted and scared and completely, utterly defeated.

"Alex has a boyfriend?"

Jimmy nodded. When he spoke, his voice came out small. Broken. A little boy again.

"Yes, sir."

He'd promised Alex. Looked him in the eye and promised to protect him. And now he was the one who needed protecting. He'd fucked up. Bad.

THE DINER WAS warm and loud and full of laughter.

They'd been there for over an hour now—pie demolished, coffee refilled twice, the waitress giving up on clearing their table. Brad was wedged into the booth between Alex and Jaime, with Susan and Thom across from them. He had color back in his face now. Susan was telling another story. Thom was adding commentary that made Jaime groan.

Alex sat back, still processing everything that had happened in the last few hours. Brad showing up. The reunion. Coming out to his oldest friend. And before all of that—just a few hours ago, though it felt like days—Jaime had proposed, and Alex had said yes.

Yes.

He was engaged. To Jaime. He was going to marry someone.

Wasn't that something older people did? People with careers and mortgages and retirement plans? He was eighteen. He'd known Jaime for three months. And yet, sitting here in this booth, watching Jaime laugh at something his father said, catching that warm look Jaime threw his way over Brad's head—it didn't feel crazy. It felt right.

He felt loved. Actually loved. Not the complicated, conditional love he'd grown up with, where affection came with expectations and approval had to be earned. This was something else. Something that didn't ask him to be different than he was.

And these people—Susan with her teasing, Thom with his quiet steadiness, Jaime with that smile that still made Alex's chest tight—they were his family now. Not instead of his real family. But *also*. His family, the one he'd chosen. The one that had chosen him back.

"I still can't believe you drove six hours," Alex was saying, shaking his head at Brad. "Without telling anyone."

"I told you." Brad almost smiled. "I just got in the car and started driving. Didn't even think about it."

"That's either very brave or very stupid," Susan said.

"Probably both," Brad admitted.

Under the table, Alex's phone buzzed against his thigh. He ignored it—probably Jimmy again, or Jason, or someone else who could wait. Tomorrow, his parents would be here. His two worlds would collide. But tonight was for this.

His phone buzzed again.

"You should probably get that," Jaime murmured, leaning forward to catch Alex's eye past Brad.

"It can wait."

"You sure?"

Alex met his gaze and smiled. "I'm sure."

JIMMY STOOD FROZEN IN HIS PARENTS' kitchen. The word was still hanging in the air.

Bill hadn't moved. For a moment, Jimmy thought he was going to explode—saw the tension coiling in his father's shoulders, the way his hands clenched at his sides.

But then something shifted. The anger drained out of his face, replaced by something worse. Something older. His eyes went distant, like he was seeing someone who wasn't in the room.

When he spoke, his voice was barely a whisper. "God. Not again."

Elizabeth looked at him sharply. "Bill?"

He didn't answer. Just stood there, hand gripping the back of his chair, knuckles white. His whole body had gone rigid—not with rage, but with something that looked almost like grief.

"Bill, I'm sure there's an explanation." Elizabeth's voice was trembling. "Jimmy must have misunderstood—"

"He didn't misunderstand." Bill's voice cracked. He turned away, one hand coming up to cover his face. "He didn't misunderstand."

"But Alex would have told us. He would have—"

"Would he?" Bill turned back, and his eyes were wet. Red-rimmed. Like something had broken open inside him. "Would he have told us, Liz? Really? After everything we—" He stopped. Shook his head. Couldn't finish.

Elizabeth stared at him. There was something in his face she'd never seen before. Something that went deeper than this moment, deeper than Alex. Some old wound she didn't know existed.

"What do you mean, 'not again'?" she asked quietly.

Bill didn't answer.

"What's wrong?" Scotty's voice broke through his sobs. He was staring at his father—at the tears, the shaking hands, the face that didn't look like Dad anymore. "Is Alex in trouble? Is he hurt?"

Jimmy couldn't stand it anymore. He pushed back from the table and walked—then ran—down the hall to his room. He slammed the door, locked it, and collapsed onto his bed.

What did I do? What did I do?

He grabbed his phone with shaking hands. Pulled up Alex's contact. Started typing.

> alex

He deleted it. Started again.

> alex I fucked up

Sent. He waited. The screen stayed dark.

please answer

Nothing.

im so sorry

Still nothing.

Jimmy pressed the call button. It rang once, twice, three times. Voicemail.

He tried again. Voicemail.

"Pick up," he whispered. "Please, Alex. Pick up."

THEY DROVE BACK to campus around ten.

The ride from the diner had been easy—Susan telling stories, Thom adding dry commentary, Brad actually laughing. Whatever had been broken in him when he arrived, something was starting to mend.

Susan and Thom dropped them off near the student center lot where Brad's car was still parked.

"We'll see you tomorrow," Susan said, pulling Alex into one of her hugs—that firm, warm embrace that made his chest tight. "Whatever happens," she murmured near his ear, "you have us. You know that, right?"

He nodded against her shoulder. "I know."

Thom shook his hand, then pulled him in for a brief hug too. "Get some rest. Big day tomorrow."

They watched the rental car disappear down the campus road. Brad jogged over to his Honda to grab his bag, and Alex and Jaime waited for him at the bottom of the path that led up to Harrison Hall. The night air was cold, their breath visible in small white clouds.

Alex's phone buzzed in his pocket.

He pulled it out, expecting Jason, or maybe something from his parents about tomorrow.

The screen showed **6 missed calls. 8 text messages.** All from Jimmy.

Alex stopped walking. The warmth of the evening—Susan's hug, Brad's laugh, the feeling of things finally coming together— drained out of him.

"Alex?" Jaime turned back. "What's wrong?"

Alex didn't answer. He was scrolling through the texts, his heart pounding harder with each one.

JIMMY:

alex

alex I fucked up

please answer

im so sorry

didnt mean to

please call me

they know

alex please

They know.

The words blurred. Alex felt the blood leave his face.

"Alex. Talk to me." Jaime was beside him now, hand on his arm.

"I have to—" Alex stepped away, toward a tree at the edge of the path. His hands were shaking as he pressed the call button.

Jimmy picked up before the first ring finished.

"Alex—" His voice was wrecked. Raw from crying.

"What happened?"

"I'm sorry, I'm so sorry, I didn't mean to—"

"Jimmy. What. Happened."

So Jimmy tried.

"They were—fuck, okay, so Dad was being a dick about the babysitter again, right? And I just—I fucking lost it, Alex, I was so pissed, and I started yelling about how I do everything and they don't even—and then I was talking about you, like how you get to—shit, I don't even know what I was saying, I was just so mad and it all came out wrong and I said something about—about you and parties and your boyfriend and I didn't even—I wasn't trying to—"

"Jimmy. Slow down."

"I can't!" His voice cracked. "I fucked up so bad, Alex. I promised you. I fucking *promised* and then I just—it slipped out and I didn't even realize until they both went quiet and Dad's face—oh God, the way he looked at me—"

"What exactly did you say?"

"I don't know! Something about—about how you're probably off partying with your boyfriend instead of studying like they think and I was just trying to say that you have a life and I don't and—fuck, I don't know, it doesn't even make sense, I was just so *angry* and then it was out and I couldn't take it back."

Alex pressed his free hand against his eyes. He was piecing it together—Jimmy bitching about being the overlooked son, comparing himself to Alex, and somewhere in all that, "boyfriend" slipping out without him even realizing.

"So you didn't... you didn't tell them I was gay?"

"No! I mean—I didn't mean to—I was just talking and then—" Jimmy's breath hitched. "But it doesn't matter because they heard it and Dad kept asking 'what boyfriend' and I couldn't—I couldn't lie, Alex. He was right there and I—"

He broke off, crying again.

"It just slipped out?" Alex asked quietly.

"I didn't mean to. I swear to God, I didn't mean to. I was so fucking pissed about my own shit that I forgot—I forgot what I was saying and—" He stopped. "And then I saw their faces."

Alex didn't say anything. He let Jimmy breathe.

"Dad just... walked away," Jimmy continued, his voice smaller now. "He went to his office and shut the door. Mom's been in their bedroom crying. Scotty's scared—he doesn't understand what's happening."

"Jimmy—"

"I'm sorry, Alex. I'm so, so sorry."

Alex opened his eyes. Across the path, Jaime was watching him, hands in his pockets, face full of quiet worry. Waiting.

Footsteps on the pavement. Brad was walking back from his car, duffel bag slung over his shoulder. He slowed when he saw Alex hunched against a tree, phone pressed to his ear.

Jaime caught his eye and held up a hand—*wait*. Brad stopped a few feet away, looking between them.

"I know you're sorry," Alex said into the phone. "I believe you."

"You do?"

"Yeah." His voice came out steadier than he felt. Inside, his chest was tight, his mind racing through everything this meant— tomorrow, his parents, the dinner—but Jimmy was crying on the other end of the line, and Scotty was scared, and Alex couldn't fall apart right now. Not yet. "It's... it's gonna be okay, Jimmy."

"How? How is it gonna be okay? I fucked everything up—"

"You didn't mean to."

"But I promised—"

"I know." Alex closed his eyes. The terror was still there— God, was it still there—but underneath it, something else. Something that felt almost like... acceptance. "But maybe this was always going to happen. Maybe I was always going to get outed, one way or another. At least this way, I know you're on my side."

Jimmy was crying again. "I am. I swear I am."

"I know."

"What are you going to do?"

Alex looked at Jaime. At the dorm behind him. At the sky full of stars he couldn't see through the campus lights.

"I don't know," he said honestly. "But I'm going to figure it out. And Jimmy—Scotty. He's too young to be worrying like this. You gotta tell him it's okay. Tell him his big brothers are gonna be fine."

"I already told him. He asked if you were gonna die." Jimmy's voice cracked on the word.

Alex's heart clenched. Scotty. Seven years old and scared his brother was going to die because of something he didn't even understand.

"Tell him I love him," Alex said quietly. "And that I'm okay. And that I'll see him soon."

Jimmy went quiet for a moment. The Robertsons didn't say things like that. Not out loud. Not to each other.

"Yeah," Jimmy finally said, his voice thick. "I will." A pause. "Alex, I'm really sorry. I know I keep saying it, but—"

"Stop apologizing. I mean it. If you say you're sorry one more time, I'm going to kick your ass when I see you."

Jimmy laughed—a wet, shaky sound. "You couldn't kick my ass. I'm taller."

"I'm meaner."

"That's true." A pause. Then another. Jimmy cleared his throat. "Alex?"

"Yeah?"

"I, uh..." Jimmy stopped. Started again. "I lo—" He couldn't get the word out. The Robertsons didn't say this. They just didn't. But he needed to. He needed Alex to know. "I love you," he finally managed, the words coming out rough and strange. "Even though you're my dorky gay brother."

The words hit Alex like a kick to the gut.

He couldn't remember the last time anyone in his family had said that to him. Maybe when he was little. Maybe never. And here was Jimmy—fifteen-year-old, foul-mouthed, pain-in-the-ass Jimmy—choking out the words like they cost him something.

Because they did. For both of them.

"I love you too." Alex's voice cracked. He meant it. God, he meant it. "Even though you're an annoying little shit who can't keep his fucking mouth shut."

Jimmy laughed—a real laugh this time, surprised out of him.

Across the path, Jaime's head snapped up. He'd heard it and his face tightened with worry—was Alex pissed? But then Alex laughed too, and Jaime's shoulders relaxed.

"Alright," Alex said, pulling himself together. "Quit jerking off and go help your little brother for once."

"Oh, fuck you," Jimmy snorted, but there was warmth in it. This was a side of Alex he'd never really known. The playful side. The brother side. All those years growing up in the same house, and they'd never had this.

"Later, Jimmy."

"Later."

The line went dead.

Alex stood there for a moment, phone clutched in his hand, feeling the weight of everything that had just changed. Then he pushed off the tree and walked back toward Jaime.

Brad was there too now, standing a few feet back, uncertain. He'd heard enough of Alex's side of the conversation to know something was very wrong.

"Hey." Jaime took Alex's hand. "You okay?"

"No." Alex squeezed his fingers. "But I will be."

Brad shifted his weight. "What happened? Is everything—"

Alex's voice was hollow. "My parents found out about me and Jaime."

Brad went still. "Shit," he said quietly. "How?"

"Jimmy. I guessed it slipped out during a fight. He didn't mean to." Alex laughed—a sharp, brittle sound. "And they're coming here tomorrow.

"Brad didn't know what to say. He looked at Jaime, who shook his head slightly—*not now.*

"Come on," Jaime said quietly, tugging Alex toward the dorm. "Let's get inside."

The three of them walked up the path together, Brad's duffel bag bumping against his hip. He kept glancing at Alex, at the devastation written across his face, and thought about his own problems—Mindy, Duke, basketball—and felt suddenly, deeply stupid for thinking any of it mattered.

This was real. This was someone's whole life, cracking open.

He didn't know how to help. But he could stay. That much, he could do.

LATER THAT NIGHT, a knock came at Alex's door.

Brad had been sitting on the edge of the bed, staring at nothing. Alex had gone upstairs to Jaime's room—said he needed a minute, needed to think. Brad understood. But he didn't know what to do with himself. He'd driven six hours to dump his problems on Alex, and now those problems felt like nothing. Mindy, Duke, basketball—who gave a shit? His best friend's life was cracking open, and Brad was just sitting here like an idiot.

He opened the door. Jaime stood in the hallway, looking almost sheepish.

"Sorry to bother you. I was wondering if I could grab Alex's sketchpad." Jaime gestured past him into the room. "His drawing always seems to put him in a good space—like nothing else exists when he's working. I thought it might help tonight, considering..."

Brad stepped aside. "Yeah, of course."

He watched Jaime cross to the desk and pick up the leather-bound sketchbook. Something tugged at a memory—Alex in middle school, hunched over a notebook at lunch, lost to the world. Alex at Brad's house, drawing in the corner while everyone else played video games. That same faraway look, like he'd slipped somewhere only he could go.

Brad had thought it was weird back then. He understood it differently now.

"Hey," Brad said as Jaime turned to leave. "Can I ask you something?"

Jaime paused in the doorway. "Yeah. Of course."

"I don't know what to do." Brad rubbed the back of his neck. "I came here because I was a mess, and Alex just—he dropped everything to help me. And now this happens, and I want to help him back, but I don't know how. And I don't want to be in the way."

"You're not in the way."

"But I don't know what I'm doing here. Should I stay? Should I go? I feel like I'm just taking up space."

Jaime was quiet for a moment. Then he stepped back into the room and closed the door behind him.

"Can I be honest with you?"

"Yeah."

"Alex is loved. He knows that. He knows you came all this way, he knows you're here for him—that matters. But the best thing you can do right now?" Jaime shrugged. "Maybe it's not trying to help him. Maybe it's helping yourself."

Brad frowned. "What do you mean?"

"You said you don't know if you want to keep playing basketball. You don't know what you're doing at Duke. That's real stuff, Brad. That's your life." Jaime paused. "Go back. Go to practice. Work on school. The semester's almost over anyway—gives you time to figure things out without quitting by accident."

"But Alex—"

"Alex will be okay." Jaime said it firmly. Not dismissive—certain. "It sucks. I'm not going to pretend it doesn't. But maybe this is a blessing in disguise?" He winced slightly. "God, that's such a cliché. But I mean it. Sooner or later, Alex was going to have to confront this. His parents, his future, all of it. He couldn't hide forever."

Brad was quiet, turning that over.

"Same goes for you," Jaime added. "You can't keep drifting. At some point, you have to decide what you actually want."

"I don't know what I want."

"Then figure it out. That's your job right now. Not standing around here feeling guilty."

Brad almost smiled. "You're pretty good at this."

"At what?"

"Giving advice. Being..." He gestured vaguely. "I don't know. Solid."

Jaime laughed—a small, tired sound. "I'm eighteen, man. I'm making this up as I go." He paused. "But I love Alex. And I think you do too, in your own way. So trust me when I say—he'll be okay. We'll figure it out."

Brad nodded slowly. "Okay."

Jaime turned to open the door. "We'll get breakfast before you head out."

"Thanks." Brad hesitated. "And thanks for—I don't know. Not making me feel like an asshole for showing up like this."

"You're not an asshole. You're a friend who needed help." Jaime clapped him on the shoulder. "Now go get some sleep. Tomorrow's going to be a long day for all of us."

IN OXFORD, Jimmy sat on Scotty's bed, his little brother curled against his side.

Scotty had stopped crying, but he was still sniffling, his face pressed into Jimmy's t-shirt. Their parents' bedroom door was closed. The house was silent except for the hum of the refrigerator.

"Is Alex going to be okay?" Scotty whispered.

"Yeah." Jimmy put his arm around his brother, pulling him closer. "Yeah, he's going to be okay."

"Promise?"

Jimmy thought about Alex's voice on the phone—scared but steady. Thought about the words he'd said: *Maybe this was always going to happen.*

"I promise," Jimmy said.

He didn't know if it was true. He didn't know what tomorrow would bring, or what their parents would do, or how any of this would end.

But he'd made a promise to his brother. Both his brothers.

And he intended to keep it.

18

Brother's Keeper

The ballroom was filling up when Alex arrived.

Parents mingled near the entrance, cocktail glasses in hand, making small talk with other parents they'd never see again. Students stood awkwardly beside them, caught between their college selves and the children they became around their families. Somewhere, a string quartet played something classical that nobody was listening to.

Alex scanned the room. No sign of his parents.

"They might not come," Jaime said quietly beside him.

"They'll come." Alex didn't know if he believed it. "My dad wouldn't miss this. He's too... proper."

Susan appeared at his elbow, pressing a glass of sparkling water into his hand. "Drink something. You look like you're about to pass out."

"I'm fine."

"You're not fine. And that's okay." She squeezed his arm. "Whatever happens tonight, you have us. You know that."

Alex nodded, but his eyes kept drifting to the entrance.

Over breakfast that morning, they'd filled Susan and Thom in on everything—Jimmy's accidental slip, the phone call, the silence from his parents since. Brad had joined them, quiet and supportive, before hugging Alex goodbye and heading back to Duke with a promise to be a phone call away.

"Let's find our table," Thom suggested. "Standing here staring at the door isn't going to help anyone."

They made their way through the crowd to Table 19 — the Stamfords' assigned spot. Alex's table was three away, at Table 22. Close enough to see. Too far to hear. He glanced at the place cards waiting for him there: *William Robertson. Elizabeth Robertson. Alexander Robertson.* Three chairs on one side, three empty on the other for a family they didn't know.

"Stay with us until they get here," Susan said, pulling out a chair for him. "No point sitting over there alone."

Alex nodded gratefully and sat between Jaime and Susan. Thom took the seat across from them, positioning himself with a clear view of the entrance.

The cocktail hour stretched on. Alex nursed his water. Jaime kept a hand on his knee under the table, steadying him. Susan made conversation with parents at nearby tables, her social instincts on autopilot. Thom watched the door.

"There," Thom said quietly.

Alex's head snapped up.

A man had just walked in — late, alone, still wearing his coat. He stood in the doorway looking around the room with the expression of someone who'd rather be anywhere else.

Bill Robertson.

No Liz.

"Where's your mother?" Jaime murmured.

"I don't know." Alex's voice came out thin. "She's not—"

He couldn't finish. Thom was already on his feet. "Stay here," he said to Jaime and Susan. "Both of you."

"Dad—" Jaime started.

"Stay here." It wasn't a suggestion.

Alex watched as Thom crossed the room, weaving between tables with the easy confidence of someone who'd navigated a thousand social situations. He intercepted Bill near the entrance, extended his hand, said something Alex couldn't hear.

Bill looked startled. Then confused. Then — something else. Not angry. Just... lost.

From Table 19, Jaime leaned forward. "What's he saying?"

The four of them watched the two men talk — Thom gesturing calmly, Bill nodding slowly, his eyes scanning the crowd.

Looking for Alex.

Alex felt his father's gaze land on him. Bill stood thirty feet away, looking right at him, and Alex couldn't read his expression at all. Not anger. Not disgust. Not even disappointment. Just... thought. Like he was working through a problem he didn't have the answer to yet.

Thom said something else. Bill nodded, not looking away from Alex.

Then Bill started walking toward Table 19.

Alex gripped the edge of the table. Jaime's hand found his under the tablecloth.

Bill stopped in front of them. He looked at Alex for a long moment. Then at Jaime. Then at Susan.

"Son."

"Dad." The word came out cracked.

Bill stood there for a moment, looking at Alex like he wasn't sure what came next. Then: "Your mother isn't coming tonight. She's... she had something else she needed to do."

Alex didn't ask what. He wasn't sure he wanted to know.

Thom had returned to the table. "Bill, why don't you sit with us until dinner starts? There's an empty chair."

Bill hesitated, then sat down heavily. He looked older than Alex remembered. Tired. Like he hadn't slept.

Because he probably hadn't.

No one spoke for a moment. Susan, ever the diplomat, tried to ease the tension. "It's good to finally meet you, Bill. Alex has told us so much about his family."

Bill nodded stiffly. "I appreciate you... looking after him."

A man in a tuxedo stepped up to the small stage at the front of the ballroom and tapped the microphone. "Good evening, everyone. If you'll please find your seats, dinner will be served shortly, followed by a short presentation." Around them, parents and students began moving toward their assigned tables.

"That's us," Susan said gently. She touched Alex's arm. "You'll be okay."

Alex stood on unsteady legs. His assigned table waited three rows away — close enough to see Jaime, too far to reach him. Bill rose too, and for a moment they just looked at each other. They walked there together, side by side but not touching, Alex feeling Jaime's eyes on his back the whole way.

The meal came in courses. Salad. Soup. Some kind of chicken that Alex couldn't taste. He pushed food around his plate while his father did the same. Bill talked, mostly. Alex listened.

From three tables away, Jaime watched them.

"He couldn't hear anything—just saw Alex's profile, his father's back, the occasional nod or shake of the head. Whatever Bill was saying, Alex seemed intent on every word. At one point, Alex's face did something complicated—surprise, then confusion, then something that looked almost like pain."

"What's happening?" Jaime's leg bounced under the table. He fidgeted with his fork, turning it over and over. "What's he telling him?"

"He's fine," Susan said softly, putting her hand on his arm. "Look at him. He's listening."

"But what if—"

"Jaime." Thom glanced over at Table 22, then back at his son. "Sometimes you need to let people work through things on their own. That can be one of the most difficult lessons in life."

Jaime understood. He hated it, but he understood. He wanted to rush over and just hold Alex. Make it better. But he couldn't. And he felt helpless.

As if reading his son's mind, Thom added while cutting a piece of chicken, "You being here for Alex is helping, Jaime. More than you know."

Jaime sat with that for a moment. It didn't make him feel better, but it was something.

"Eat your dinner," Thom said gently. "They're just doing their work. Probably needed to have this moment away from home for years now." He took a bite. "It'll be okay."

Jaime tried. He really did. But every few seconds, his eyes drifted back to Table 22, to the two figures leaning slightly toward each other, to the conversation he couldn't hear and couldn't stop imagining.

At one point, Alex looked like he might cry. At another, Bill pressed his hand over his eyes. Something was happening over there — something big — but Jaime could only watch from a distance, helpless.

Then, before the servers had even cleared the main course, they stood.

"Where are they going?" Jaime was half out of his chair before Thom's hand caught his arm.

"Sit down."

"But Dad — they're leaving. The presentations haven't even started—"

"They're not fighting. Look at them."

Jaime looked. His father was right — Bill wasn't storming out, and Alex wasn't trailing behind in tears. They were walking together, side by side, heading toward the ballroom doors. Alex glanced back once, caught Jaime's eye, and gave a small nod.

I'm okay. I need to do this.

"I should follow them," Jaime said.

"No." Susan's voice was firm. "Your father's right. This is their conversation."

"But what if—"

Thom stood, placing his napkin on the table. "I'll keep an eye out. You stay here with your mother."

"Dad—"

"Stay. Here."

Susan's eyes pleaded with her husband. *Is Alex going to be okay?*

Thom gave her a small nod, then walked toward the doors, moving casually, like he was just stretching his legs.

Susan put her hand over Jaime's. "He's going to be okay. Whatever happens, he has us. He knows that."

Jaime watched his father disappear through the doors. Then he stared at his plate and tried to remember how to breathe.

THE CORRIDOR outside the ballroom was quiet.

Hotel art lined the walls — bland landscapes, generic still lifes. Bill walked until he found a bench at the far end, away from the noise and the crowds.

They sat down together. Not touching, but close.

Thom had followed at a distance. He didn't have to go far — they'd stopped at a bench visible from the corridor entrance. He pretended to study a sculpture near the restrooms, keeping one eye on them. Bill didn't look angry. Alex didn't look scared. Alex actually looked... eager. Like he wanted to hear whatever Bill was telling him.

On the bench, Bill stared at the far wall.

"I need to tell you something," he said. "Something I should have told you a long time ago."

Alex waited.

"I had a brother. His name was Chris."

Alex blinked. A brother? His father had a brother? He'd

never heard anything about an uncle. Not once in eighteen years. This was not what he'd expected — not a lecture, not anger, not disappointment. This was something else entirely.

BILL TOLD HIM EVERYTHING.

About Chris — four years younger, different as night and day. The Guess jeans and too much mascara. The underground dance parties with his best friend Steve. The way Bill had promised to protect him, told him it was okay with him, that's what big brothers do.

"I knew about him and Steve," Bill said, still not looking at Alex. "Never said anything directly, but... I knew."

Alex sat very still. He'd never heard his father talk like this. Never heard him talk about anything before, really.

"The night it happened, they went to some party in Columbus. A rave, Chris called it. They were coming out when some guys—" Bill shook his head. "Chris was beaten pretty badly. Steve too. The police found them in an alley behind the club."

Alex felt his stomach drop. "What happened?" His voice came out barely above a whisper.

"My father drove us to the station to pick him up. And when he figured out what Chris was — what Chris and Steve were to each other—" Bill's jaw tightened. "He told Chris not to come home."

Alex's breath caught. "He kicked him out?"

"Right there. In the police station. In front of everyone." Bill finally looked up, and his eyes were wet. "And I didn't say anything. I just stood there. I'd promised to protect him, and when it mattered — when he needed me — I just stood there."

Alex thought about Jimmy's phone call last night. About his little brother crying, apologizing, promising to protect him even though he was the one who'd slipped.

"What happened to him? To Chris?"

"I don't really know." The admission seemed to cost Bill something. "I think he stayed with friends for a while. Then... I heard he left. Went somewhere. I never..." He pressed his hand over his eyes. "I never looked for him. I was too much of a coward."

Alex didn't know what to say. His whole life, his father had been a monument — solid, certain, immovable. And now here he was, crumbling on a hotel bench, telling stories about a brother Alex never knew existed.

"I watched you grow up." Bill dropped his hand, looked at Alex with something raw in his face. "And every year, you looked more like him. Acted more like him. The drawing. The sensitivity. The way you were with Jason." He shook his head. "I knew. I think I always knew. And I was so afraid—" His voice broke. "I was so afraid you'd end up like Chris. That someone would hurt you. That I'd lose you the way I lost him."

"So you just... pretended not to see?"

"I thought if I didn't acknowledge it, maybe it would go away. Maybe you'd be different. Maybe you'd be... safe."

The word hung between them. *Safe.* All those years of silence, of careful distance, of never quite connecting — it hadn't been rejection. It had been fear.

"I'm not angry that you're gay," Bill said quietly. "I'm angry that you felt you had to hide it. That I made you feel like you had to hide it." He paused. "That's on me, son. Not you."

Alex felt tears building behind his eyes. He blinked them back.

"Why didn't you ever tell me? About Chris?"

"Because I was ashamed." Bill said it simply, like a fact. "I abandoned my brother when he needed me most. I went along with my father because I was young and scared and I wanted to keep the peace. And I've lived with that for thirty years." He looked at Alex — really looked at him. "I don't want you to live with that. I don't want you to ever feel like you have to hide who you are. Not from me. Not from anyone."

Alex thought about everything — the years of silence, the distance, the fear he'd carried for as long as he could remember. And underneath it all, his father, carrying his own fear. His own guilt. His own brother-shaped wound that never healed.

"I'm sorry," Bill said. "For all of it."

Alex nodded slowly. It wasn't enough. It wasn't nearly enough.

They sat in silence for a moment. The weight of Chris's story hung between them. Alex watched his father — this broken man who'd been carrying guilt for thirty years — and felt his anger softening into something more complicated.

"Is he still alive?" Alex asked quietly. "Chris. Do you know?"

Bill shook his head slowly. "I tried to find him a few times over the years. Especially when... when that disease started showing up everywhere. I was terrified he might've..." He couldn't finish. "I think he went out west. San Francisco, maybe. Or LA." He shook his head. "Can't blame him. What was there for him here? After what we did?"

The *we* landed heavy. Bill wasn't just talking about his father anymore.

"I regret it," Bill said quietly. "Every day. Not knowing where he is. What I did. What I didn't do." He finally looked at Alex. "I can't change any of that. But I can change how things go with you."

Alex stared at the wall, processing. Part of him wanted to hate his father. For Chris. For standing there and saying nothing. For thirty years of silence. For letting Alex grow up terrified of the same thing happening to him.

He wanted to hate him. He tried to.

But he couldn't. Because sitting next to him wasn't the monument he'd grown up fearing. It was just a man. A broken one. Someone who'd made terrible choices and lived with them every day since. Someone who was trying — clumsily, imperfectly — to do better.

Alex had been trying not to think about it. But now, in the silence, it surfaced.

"Mom didn't come."

"No."

"Why?"

Bill rubbed his face with both hands. "She's at the Mitchells'. Talking to Jenn."

"What?"

A pause. "She thinks Jason made you this way."

Alex stood up.

"She thinks *what*?"

"I tried to talk her out of it. She wouldn't—"

"Are you kidding me?" Alex was pacing now, his voice rising. "She's not here — she's not at this dinner, not talking to me, not trying to understand any of this — because she's at Jason's house? Blaming him?"

Down the corridor, Thom looked up from the sculpture he'd been pretending to study. He straightened slightly, watching. Ready.

"Alex, your mother is scared. She doesn't know how to—"

"Don't." Alex turned on him. "Don't make excuses for her."

Bill went quiet.

"You just told me about an uncle I never knew existed. An uncle you walked away from and never looked for. Thirty years, Dad. Thirty years of pretending he didn't exist." Alex's hands were shaking. "And you know what? I get it. I don't like it, but I get it. You were young. You were scared. You've been carrying that guilt ever since."

Bill said nothing.

"But her?" Alex's voice cracked. "She's not scared. She's not confused. She's choosing this. She's choosing Pastor Davis and his bullshit over her own son."

"That's not fair—"

"It's completely fair." Alex stopped pacing, facing his father.

"If she wanted to understand, she'd be here. Right now. Talking to me. But she's not. She's over at my best friend's house telling his mom that Jason made me gay." He laughed — a sharp, bitter sound. "How fucked up is that?"

Bill stared at him.

He'd never heard Alex speak like this. Never heard him curse, never seen this kind of raw fury in his quiet, careful son. Part of him wanted to reprimand him — he hadn't raised his children to talk this way. But he also knew Alex was in a moment. And it wasn't like he'd never heard these words before.

Chris used to talk just like this. The same fire. The same way of cutting straight to the truth and refusing to look away.

His son was more like his brother than like him. Bill had always known it. He just hadn't let himself see it until now.

"I know Jenn won't take her shit," Alex continued, his voice quieter now but still sharp. "Jenn's tougher than Mom will ever be. But Jason — God, Jason's going to have to deal with this. He's going to find out my mother came to his house and blamed him for something that has nothing to do with him." Alex pressed his hands over his eyes. "It's humiliating. For all of us."

Down the hall, Thom had taken a few steps closer. Not intruding. Just present. Watching.

Bill tried again. "Your mother loves you. She just—"

"Then why isn't she here?" Alex dropped his hands. His eyes were wet. "Why does she listen to that pastor more than she listens to me? More than she listens to you?" He shook his head. "If she really loved me, she'd be sitting on this bench right now. Not running around Oxford trying to find someone to blame."

Bill had no answer for that.

Alex stood there for a long moment, his chest heaving. And then something in him just... collapsed.

He sat back down on the bench, hard. Put his head in his hands. And started to cry.

Not quietly. Not the kind of tears you could blink away.

These were the sobs of someone who'd been holding everything in for too long — years, maybe — and finally couldn't hold it anymore.

"I don't understand," he said to no one. "I don't understand why this is so hard. Why I feel more welcome in Jaime's family than my own. Why his parents treat me more like a son than..." He couldn't finish.

Bill felt the words land like punches. Each one true. Each one earned.

He thought about the distance he'd kept for eighteen years. The conversations he'd avoided. The way he'd let Liz handle anything emotional because he didn't know how. All those years of treating Alex the way he'd treated Chris — keeping him at arm's length, pretending not to see, hoping it would all just work out somehow.

This whole family charade was being turned upside down. And Bill knew it had started long before Alex was even born. Before he'd married Liz. Before he'd learned to bury everything that hurt too much to look at.

Alex was still crying. His shoulders shook with it.

Bill didn't know what to do. When the boys were little — when they fell down and scraped their knees, or threw tantrums the way kids do — he'd always let Liz handle it. She was better at feelings. He wasn't built for this.

But Liz wasn't here. And his son needed something. Needed him.

Awkwardly, Bill reached over and placed his hand on Alex's back. He rubbed it slightly — small circles, the way he'd seen Liz do a thousand times. He didn't say anything. Didn't know what to say.

Alex kept crying. But after a while, the sobs slowed. His breathing steadied.

He noticed his father's hand. The clumsy attempt at comfort.

And he realized — this was as good as it got. This was all Bill Robertson knew how to give.

Alex lifted his head, wiping his face with his sleeve. His eyes drifted down the corridor.

Thom was still there. Standing near the sculpture, pretending to read the placard. He hadn't come closer — hadn't intruded. But he was there. Watching. Protecting. The way he'd been doing all night.

Their eyes met.

Thom gave a small nod. Almost imperceptible. *I'm here. You're okay.*

Alex felt something shift in his chest. He had his father beside him — trying, failing, trying again. And he had another father figure down the hall, silently looking out for him. Two very different men. Two very different kinds of love.

Maybe that was enough. Maybe it had to be.

He turned back to Bill.

"Dad?"

"Yeah?"

Alex kept his eyes forward. Couldn't look at him. Not for this.

"I love you." His voice was rough, scraped raw. "I don't understand why it's all this way. But I love you."

Bill was quiet for a long moment. His hand was still on Alex's back — he hadn't moved it. Hadn't known what else to do with it.

"I..." He stopped. Tried again. "I love you too, son."

The words came out rough. Unpracticed. Like something he'd kept locked away so long he'd almost forgotten where he put the key.

No hug. No dramatic moment. Just two Robertson men, sitting side by side on a hotel bench, saying words they'd never said before.

Alex thought about Jaime. About the family they might build someday. The words he'd say to his own children every single day until he was blue in the face. *I love you. I'm proud of you. You're perfect exactly as you are.*

He'd do it differently. He'd do it better.

But for now, sitting next to his father in a quiet corridor, hearing those three words for the first time in his life—

It was a start.

JAIME HAD BARELY TOUCHED his dessert.

Around them, the evening continued as if nothing was wrong. A dean had taken the stage to share statistics about the freshman class — retention rates, academic achievements, the usual self-congratulation. Parents laughed at the right moments, applauded on cue. At a nearby table, a mother was showing photos on her phone while her daughter groaned with embarrassment.

Susan had given up trying to make small talk with the other parents at their table. She kept one hand on Jaime's arm, grounding him.

"They've been gone a long time," Jaime said quietly.

"That's probably good. It means they're actually talking."

"Or something's gone horribly wrong."

"Jaime." Susan's voice was gentle but firm. "Your father's out there. He'll come get us if anything—"

"I know. I know." Jaime pushed a piece of cake around his plate. "I just hate not knowing."

The dean finished his remarks. Applause rippled through the room. Someone clinked a glass. Laughter from the table behind them.

Susan watched her son — the way his leg bounced under the table, the way his eyes kept drifting to the doors. She'd never seen him like this. Her bright, confident boy, reduced to anxious waiting.

"He's lucky to have you," she said.

Jaime looked at her.

"Alex. He's lucky." She squeezed his arm. "Whatever's happening out there — he knows you're here. That matters more than you realize."

Jaime nodded but didn't respond. His eyes went back to the doors.

A few minutes later, Thom slipped back into his seat.

"Well?" Susan whispered.

"I think they're going to be okay."

Jaime's head snapped up. "What happened? Is he—"

"I don't know what they talked about." Thom put his hand on his son's shoulder. "But whatever it was, I think they needed to have it."

The ballroom doors opened.

Bill walked in first, Alex a step behind. Bill's eyes were red-rimmed, but his shoulders were straighter than when he'd walked in alone. Alex scanned the room, found Table 19, found Jaime.

Their eyes met.

Alex gave a small smile. Not *I'm fine.* Not *everything's perfect.*

Just *I'm okay. We're going to be okay.*

Jaime felt something loosen in his chest. He wanted to go to him — cross the room, pull him into his arms, ask what the hell had happened out there. But he stayed in his seat. This wasn't the moment.

Later. They'd have later.

PART IV

RESOLUTION

19

Prayers

Jenn was restocking the international foods aisle when she heard footsteps behind her.

It was a little after six on a Friday evening. Her shift ran eleven to seven-thirty, and the last hour and a half was always the quietest. Most folks had already done their shopping, headed home to start dinner or out to whatever plans the weekend held. She'd have the place practically to herself until close.

She was looking forward to a quiet night. Leftovers, maybe some TV. Jason had been quieter since Alex left for college — more time alone in his room, sketching or talking to friends online. But lately he'd been coming by the store more often, hanging around when Brandon was working. The new kid she'd hired part-time a few months back. She liked seeing Jason making a new friend, even if she had to shoo him away sometimes to let Brandon actually get his work done.

"Jenn?"

She turned, a jar of tahini in her hand.

Elizabeth Robertson stood at the end of the aisle, clutching her purse against her chest like a shield.

"Liz." Jenn set the jar on the shelf. "Didn't hear you come in."

"I'm sorry. I didn't mean to startle you."

"It's fine." Jenn studied her for a moment. Liz looked drawn, pale. Not her usual put-together self. "What brings you in? We close in about an hour."

Liz's eyes darted around the empty aisle. "I was hoping we could talk. About the boys."

"The boys?"

"Alex and Jason." Liz's voice dropped. "Is everything... is everything okay? With them?"

Jenn felt her guard go up. She kept her expression neutral. "Far as I know. Why?"

"Could we go somewhere more private? I don't want to—" Liz glanced toward the front of the store where Margie was working the register. "It's a sensitive matter."

Jenn wiped her hands on her apron. "Break room's upstairs. Follow me."

THE BREAK ROOM was small and windowless — a card table, a few plastic chairs, a vending machine humming in the corner. Jenn fed some quarters into it and retrieved a Diet Coke.

"You want one?"

Liz shook her head, settling gingerly into one of the chairs. She set her purse on the table but kept one hand on it, like she might need to flee at any moment.

Jenn sat across from her and popped the tab on her soda. Took a long sip. Waited.

She and Liz had gone to school together — same graduating class at Oxford High, though they'd never been close. Different crowds. Jenn ran with the art kids, the drama club. Liz was quieter, more serious. Youth group on Wednesdays, church on Sundays. They'd nodded at each other in the halls, partnered on a lab assignment once in sophomore biology. That was about it.

After graduation, their paths had diverged entirely. Liz married Bill Robertson right out of high school, settled into a nice house, had three boys. The picture of a proper family. Jenn had taken a different route — married young, divorced younger, left to raise Jason alone when his father decided a family was too much responsibility.

She'd felt the judgment from certain corners of town. The church crowd, mostly. Single mothers weren't exactly celebrated in Oxford. She'd catch the looks sometimes — pity masked as concern, disapproval dressed up as prayer requests. Liz had never been outright cruel about it, but she'd never been warm either. They existed in parallel, their sons the only real connection between them.

"So." Jenn set down her soda. "What's this about?"

Liz took a breath. Started. Stopped. Started again.

"I'm not sure how to say this."

"Take your time."

"It's just — Bill and I, we've been concerned. About Alex. About some of the... the influences he might be experiencing."

"Influences."

"At school. The people he's been spending time with." Liz smoothed her skirt with trembling hands. "We're worried he might be... confused. About certain things."

Jenn took another sip of her Diet Coke. Let the silence stretch.

"Jimmy mentioned something," Liz continued, her voice barely above a whisper. "About Alex and... and a friend of his. A particular friend. And we're just concerned that maybe—"

Jenn felt the pieces fall into place. A particular friend. Confused. Influences. She thought about Alex at the restaurant a few weeks ago—the panic on his face when she'd said 'you two are good together,' the way Jaime had stepped in because Alex couldn't find the words himself. About Jaime. About how scared he was to tell his parents.

Jimmy must have seen something. Or heard something. And now here was Liz, unable to even say it directly.

"Does Alex know you know?"

Liz blinked. "I'm sorry?"

"Have you talked to him about this? Whatever Jimmy told you?"

"Well, no. Not exactly. Bill's at the school for the parent dinner tonight, but I thought it might be better if I—

"You didn't go?"

Liz's cheeks flushed. "I felt it was important to address certain matters first. To understand the full picture before—"

"Liz." Jenn set down her soda. "Is this really a surprise to you?"

"What do you mean?"

"Alex. What Jimmy told you. Is this honestly the first time you've wondered?"

Liz's mouth opened. Closed. Her fingers tightened on her purse strap.

"I don't know what you're implying."

"I'm not implying anything. I'm asking. You've known that boy his whole life. Raised him. Did you really never notice anything?"

The silence that followed told Jenn everything she needed to know.

"That's what I thought." Jenn leaned back in her chair. "So what is it you're really here to talk about?"

Liz seemed to gather herself. When she spoke again, her voice had shifted — steadier, more practiced. Like she'd rehearsed this part.

"I know this is a sensitive topic. And I want you to know that I'm approaching this from a place of love and concern. For both our sons."

Here it comes, Jenn thought.

"Alex and Jason have always been close. Since they were children. And I've always appreciated what a good friend Jason has been to him." Liz paused. "But I can't help wondering if perhaps... if some of Jason's own struggles might have influenced Alex in ways that—"

"Hold on." Jenn held up a hand. "Are you saying what I think you're saying?"

"I'm not accusing anyone of anything. I'm simply suggesting that perhaps Jason's... perspective... might have shaped how Alex sees certain things. Young people are impressionable, and when they're exposed to certain ideas—"

"Certain ideas."

"You know what I mean." Liz's voice dropped to nearly a whisper. "These kinds of... inclinations. They can be... catching. If a young person is around someone who's already struggling with those temptations—"

"You think my son made your son gay."

Liz flinched like she'd been slapped.

"That's what you're saying, isn't it?" Jenn kept her voice level. "That Jason somehow infected Alex with gayness. Like it's a cold."

"I didn't say—"

"You didn't have to." Jenn stood up. Walked to the vending machine. Stood there for a moment with her back to Liz, collecting herself.

"I want you to know," Liz continued behind her, "that I'm only bringing this up because I care. As a Christian woman, I feel it's my duty to address these things while there's still time. While the boys are still young enough to be guided back to the right path. The church has programs that can help with these kinds of struggles. There are resources available if we act now, before—"

"Before what?" Jenn turned around. "Before it becomes permanent? Before they're too far gone to save?"

"I know you might not understand, but this is about their souls. Their eternal—"

"Let me stop you right there." Jenn walked back to the table but didn't sit. "I appreciate you coming here. It's rare we ever really talk, you and me."

Liz looked momentarily hopeful. "I'm glad you understand—"

"I didn't say I understood. I said I appreciate you coming." Jenn braced her hands on the back of the chair. "Because now I understand why we don't talk. And why Alex was afraid to tell you any of this himself."

The hope in Liz's face curdled into something else.

"Like it or not, Liz, your son is gay. I've known since he visited a few weeks ago—saw it plain as day, even if he was too scared to say it at first." Jenn watched the color drain from Liz's face. "He was in tears, Liz. Shaking. Too terrified to say the words to his own parents — the people who should love and support him most. Do you understand what that means? Your own child was more afraid of you than he was of me."

"I never—"

"And it's not something my son 'brought home.' Jason and Alex have been best friends since before either of them could ride a bicycle. I practically raised Alex in my house as much as you raised Jason in yours. I've watched them both grow up. Find their way. Make mistakes." Jenn's voice hardened. "And you know what I did through all of it? I talked with them. Not to them, Liz. With them. I let them figure things out and I tried to be there when they needed me. Both of them."

"This isn't the same—"

"Forget the gay thing for a minute." Jenn saw how Liz flinched at the word, like it burned her ears. "Just look at them, Liz. Really look. Alex and Jason are both creative. Artistic. In our day, we would have called them 'artsy.' Remember that word? Remember what we used to say about boys like that?"

Liz's face went very still.

"We'd call them names, Liz. We'd tease them. Mock them behind their backs. All the things kids do when they don't understand something." Jenn paused. "I did it. I was stupid and cruel and I didn't think twice about it. And you did it too, Liz. Maybe not out loud — you were always quiet — but you knew. When those boys walked by and everyone snickered, you'd look away. You'd walk to the other side of the hall so you didn't have to be near them. Remember that?"

Liz's eyes dropped to her lap.

"Those boys moved away, eventually. Every one of them. Left town as soon as they could get out. And we all thought, good riddance, right? If they're not here, we don't have to think about 'that stuff.'" Jenn did air quotes with her fingers. "Made it easier."

"This isn't the same situation—"

"It's exactly the same situation." Jenn sat back down, leaning forward across the table. "Our boys grew up to be like those kids we ignored. Did you make Alex this way? Did I push Jason into it? Of course not. We both tried to give them good homes. Teach them right from wrong."

"I didn't teach Alex to be..." Liz couldn't finish the sentence.

"No. You didn't. And neither did I. But we also didn't make them any particular way. They're just growing into who they've always been." Jenn held Liz's gaze. "So what do you want, Liz? Do you want them to move away like those boys from high school? Disappear so you don't have to think about it? Is that what you're hoping for? Make the 'problem' go away?"

"Of course not. I just want Alex to—" Liz stopped. Swallowed. "I just want my son to be—"

She couldn't say it. Couldn't find a way to make it sound less ugly than it was.

"You want my son to stop making your son gay?" Jenn supplied. "You want Alex to be straight? Is that how you think this works?"

"The church has programs." Liz's voice was almost pleading now. "There are ways to address these... struggles. Counselors who specialize in—"

"Pray-the-gay-away camps?" Jenn laughed, but there was no

humor in it. "Liz, that's exactly why Alex was crying when he came out. That's exactly what he was afraid of. That his own mother would try to fix him like he's broken." She shook her head. "You might as well pray for him to have blue eyes. This is who he is. All Jason ever did was be his friend."

Something shifted in Liz's face. The soft, pleading look hardened. She picked up her purse and stood.

"I was hoping you'd understand," she said quietly. "But I see now that was too much to expect. I'll have to insist that Jason stay away from my son."

Jenn laughed out loud.

Liz stared at her, startled.

"They're both adults, Liz. You might as well insist they learn French. Or become lawyers." Jenn leaned back in her chair. "They're going to make their own decisions about their own lives. It's up to us to either support them and help guide them, or get out of their way. That's it. Those are the only choices we've got."

Liz's face shuttered. She turned and walked toward the stairs without another word.

"Liz."

She stopped at the doorway. Didn't turn around.

"I'll be praying for you."

Liz's shoulders stiffened. Then she was gone, her footsteps echoing down the stairs.

Jenn sat alone in the break room for a long time, staring at her Diet Coke, her hands shaking.

"Damn," she said softly to the empty room.

20

Homeward

The drive to Oxford took just under two hours.

Alex kept both hands on the wheel, eyes on the gray November highway. The fields stretched out on either side — brown and bare, waiting for winter. Jaime sat beside him, quieter than usual.

A week and a half ago, his dad had called. Invited Jaime for Thanksgiving. Personally.

"You're quiet," Jaime said.

"Just thinking about that phone call."

"Still?"

"My dad sounded... off. Like, uncertain. I've never heard him like that."

The call had been short. His dad clearing his throat, then: "Your mother and I would like you to come home for Thanksgiving. And we'd like you to bring Jaime. It's time he met the rest of the family."

Your mother and I. Alex knew better. This was his dad's doing. His mom would never have suggested it.

"You sure about this?" Jaime asked.

"No."

"That's reassuring."

Alex almost smiled. "My dad's a pragmatist. Rip the bandaid off. Deal with it."

"Wonder where you get it from," Jaime said.

Alex glanced at him. "What's that supposed to mean?"

"Nothing." Jaime smiled slightly. "Just — you're more like him than you think."

Alex turned back to the road. Maybe. He didn't know if that was a good thing or not.

"And your mom?" Jaime asked.

Alex's grip tightened on the wheel. "No idea."

"Your dad didn't say anything about—"

"Just that they wanted us to come. That's it." He stared at the road. "She could have Pastor Davis waiting in the living room to talk about my 'lifestyle choices.' I don't know."

"Alex—"

"That's the worst part. Not knowing. If she'd just yell at me or whatever, at least I'd know."

Jaime was quiet for a moment. "What do you think's gonna happen?"

"I don't know. Maybe she ignores it. Pretends everything's normal. We eat turkey and nobody talks about anything." He shook his head. "Maybe that's worse, actually."

They drove in silence for a while. The highway stretched ahead, flat and endless.

"Why are you doing this?" Jaime asked quietly. "Really?"

Alex took a breath. "Because if they're going to throw me out, I want them to just do it. Get it over with. This waiting around, not knowing where I stand — it's killing me."

"And if they don't throw you out?"

"Then I guess we eat turkey." Alex glanced over. "Look, my dad took a step. He called. He invited you. That's huge for him. I feel like I owe him something back. Showing up is the least I can do."

Jaime reached over and put his hand on Alex's knee. Didn't say anything. Just left it there.

The Oxford exit appeared ahead. Alex put on his turn signal. "Ready?" he asked.

"No," Jaime said. "Let's go anyway."

THE ROBERTSON HOUSE looked exactly the same.

Alex pulled into the driveway and sat there for a moment, engine idling. The same beige siding. The same brown shutters. The same basketball hoop over the garage that Jimmy still used.

But everything was different now.

They were halfway up the walk when the front door burst open. "ALEX!"

Scotty hit him at full speed, arms wrapping around his waist, face buried in his coat. Alex staggered back, then laughed and hugged him tight.

"Hey, buddy. Miss me?"

"You were gone forever!"

"It's only been a few months."

"That's forever!" Scotty pulled back and looked up at him. Then his gaze shifted to Jaime. Suddenly shy, he pressed closer to Alex's side.

"Scotty, this is my friend Jaime."

Jaime crouched down so they were eye level. "Hey there. I've heard a lot about you. Alex says you're the coolest seven-year-old in Ohio."

"I'm almost eight," Scotty said quietly.

"Even cooler." Jaime smiled. "I brought you something. It's in my bag. Want to help me carry it inside?"

Scotty's eyes widened. He looked up at Alex for permission.

"Go ahead."

Scotty grabbed Jaime's hand and pulled him toward the car. A minute later, they were walking back — Scotty bouncing beside him, clutching a Lego box to his chest and grinning ear to ear.

"He's good with kids."

Alex turned. Jimmy was standing on the porch, hands in his pockets.

"Yeah. He is."

They looked at each other for a long moment. Jimmy seemed older somehow. Tired. Like he'd been carrying something heavy.

"Hey," Jimmy said.

"Hey."

"I'm sorry. For everything. I know we talked on the phone, but I wanted to say it in person."

"I know. We're okay."

"Yeah?"

Alex climbed the steps and pulled his brother into a hug. Jimmy stiffened — the Robertsons didn't do this — but Alex held on anyway. He'd learned to appreciate hugs. To want them. And he was giving them out now whether his family was ready or not.

After a moment, Jimmy relaxed into it.

"We're okay," Alex said quietly. "I promise."

When they pulled apart, Jimmy blinked fast, looking away. "Your boyfriend's being kidnapped by a seven-year-old."

Alex looked back. Scotty was tugging Jaime toward the house, already chattering about where they'd put the new Lego set and how it was the exact one he needed to finish the Death Star.

"He can handle it."

BILL MET them at the door.

He looked different than he had at the dinner — less worn, more present. When he saw Jaime, he extended his hand.

"Good to see you again, son."

"You too, Mr. Robertson."

"Bill." He shook Jaime's hand firmly. "Call me Bill."

Okay, Alex thought. *This might... work.*

"Where's Mom?" he asked.

"Kitchen. She's been working on dinner since six this morning." Bill stepped aside. "C'mon. Let's get you boys settled."

THE LIVING ROOM filled up quickly.

"Come on, Uncle Jaime!" Scotty tugged at Jaime's hand, pulling him toward the back of the house. "Come on, Uncle Jaime!" Scotty tugged at Jaime's hand, pulling him toward the back of the house. "I gotta show you what I already got done!"

Uncle Jaime. Alex saw his dad blink. Jimmy's eyebrows went up. But nobody corrected him.

Jimmy trailed after them — normally too old, too cool for his little brother's toys, but something about Jaime made it okay.

Alex stood in the living room, watching them go.

"She's in the kitchen," Bill said quietly from his La-Z-Boy. "If you want to talk to her."

Alex took a breath. "Yeah. Okay."

THE KITCHEN SMELLED like sage and butter.

Liz stood at the counter, her back to the doorway, chopping carrots with mechanical precision. The turkey was already in the oven. Pots simmered on the stove.

She knew he was there — he could tell by the slight stiffening of her shoulders — but she didn't turn around.

"Hi, Mom."

"Alex." She didn't turn around. "How was the drive?"

"Fine. Easy."

"Good. That's good." She moved to the celery. "Dinner should be ready around four. Your father said he'd handle the mashed potatoes, but you know how he is in the kitchen."

"Yeah."

Silence. Just the knife against the cutting board. The bubble of something on the stove.

Alex waited. Hoping she'd turn around. Hoping she'd say something — anything — about what had happened. About Jaime, sitting in the other room with her youngest son.

"Is there anything I can help with?" he finally asked.

"No, honey. I've got it under control."

Honey. The word was careful. Practiced.

"Mom—"

"There's soda in the fridge if you want one. Or I can make coffee."

"I'm fine."

"Okay." She kept her eyes on the cutting board. "Your father's probably wondering where you went."

Alex stood there for another moment, watching her back. Waiting for something that wasn't coming.

"Okay," he said. "I'll be in the living room."

"Okay, honey."

He grabbed a Coke from the fridge and walked out.

BILL GLANCED up when Alex came back. Didn't say anything. Didn't have to.

Alex sat down on the couch. "She's busy."

"Yeah."

The Lions were down by six. Thanksgiving tradition. Bill tried to focus on the game.

But he kept glancing at his son.

Alex had his Coke in his hand but hadn't touched it. He was

staring at the TV, but he wasn't watching. Wasn't really there at all. Just... empty.

Bill shifted in his chair. Tried to focus on the game.

Down the hall, Scotty was giggling uncontrollably. Jaime seemed to be tickling him, and Jimmy was laughing at it all. Life happening back there while his oldest son sat here fading into the couch.

Bill knew that look. He'd seen it before.

On Chris. The night before party. That same hollowness — like he was already gone, even while sitting right there.

Bill gripped the armrest. Thirty years, and he still remembered.

He'd done nothing then. Told himself it wasn't his business. Told himself Chris would figure it out. And then Chris was gone, and Bill spent the next three decades not knowing if his brother was alive or dead.

He wouldn't make that mistake again.

"I should check on those mashed potatoes," he said, pushing himself up.

Alex didn't respond.

LIZ WAS STILL CHOPPING when Bill walked into the kitchen.

"Thought I'd get started on the potatoes," he said.

"They're in the pantry. I already washed them."

"Good."

He retrieved the pot, filled it with water, set it on the stove. Let the silence stretch.

"Alex seems good," he said finally.

She didn't answer.

"Jaime's good with the boys. Scotty's already attached. Even Jimmy's warming up."

"That's nice."

He set down the peeler. "Liz."

"I'm trying, Bill." Her voice was tight. "I'm being civil. I'm being polite. What else do you want?"

"I want you to look at him."

"I am looking at him."

"No. You're hiding back here so you don't have to face him."

"I'm making Thanksgiving dinner. Someone has to."

"Liz." He moved closer, lowered his voice. "We talked about this. About Chris."

She flinched. Set down the knife.

"I still can't believe you never told me," she said quietly. "All these years."

"I know."

"I feel like I don't even know you anymore." She turned around. Her eyes were red. "A brother. A whole person you just... never mentioned."

"I was ashamed. I was a coward. I didn't know how to—"

"And now you want me to just accept this? Accept that our son is..." She couldn't say it.

"I want you to try."

"I am trying."

"No. You're going through the motions." He took a breath. "Liz, when I look at Alex — when I see him sitting out there, staring at nothing — I see Chris. I see my brother the night before everything fell apart."

"Bill—"

"I don't even know if Chris is alive. Thirty years of not knowing because I was too scared to look. Too much of a coward to find out what happened to my own brother." His voice cracked. "I won't do that again. I can't."

"This isn't the same. Alex isn't going to—"

"Isn't going to what? Disappear? End up God knows where because his own family couldn't accept him?"

Liz stared at him. This wasn't the man she knew. The steady one. The rock.

"Why does this have to be so hard?" she whispered. "Why can't things be like they used to?"

"Because our son is gay. That's the reality. We can deal with it or we can lose him."

"What about Pastor Davis talking to him?"

"Pastor Davis isn't that good, and you know it. And those church ladies, getting into everyone's business..." Bill shook his head. "I don't care what they think, Liz. I care about our son."

"That boy has him all confused. If Alex had never met—"

"That boy has a name. Jaime. And he seems like a good kid."

"He might be a nice boy, but that doesn't change—"

"Change what? That we won't have grandkids? That you can't hold your head up at church?"

"You know what I mean, Bill. Just because your brother got himself—"

"He didn't get himself anything." Bill's voice went hard. "Our father kicked him out. I let it happen. I had no guts to stand up and say it wasn't right. And I've lived with that ever since."

Liz saw something shift in his face. This wasn't the Bill she knew. He was hurt. Broken.

"I love you, Liz. I married you. But I won't let you do to Alex what I did to Chris."

Her face crumpled. "That's not fair."

"None of this is fair. But that boy out there is our son. And he's hurting. And there's another boy in the back room playing Legos with our kids who clearly loves him." He paused. "That has to count for something."

"I don't know if I can do this, Bill. I don't know how."

"I'm not asking you to suddenly pretend everything's fine. Just... try. That's all."

Liz turned back to the counter, gripping the edge. Her shoulders shook.

Bill stood there, not knowing what else to say.

• • •

ALEX HEARD IT ALL.

He'd gotten up to use the bathroom but stopped when he heard his father's voice — low, urgent, nothing like his usual calm.

He stood just out of sight, back pressed against the hallway.

I won't let you do to Alex what I did to Chris.

He'd never heard his parents argue. Not once. Not like this. His dad's voice breaking. His mom crying. All because of him.

Tears streamed down his face.

Down the hall, the laughter continued—Scotty's delighted shrieks, Jimmy's voice joining in. A world away.

Alex had Jaime. He had Jason. He was building something — people who saw him and accepted him for who he was.

But standing here, in his own house, listening to his parents fight about whether to keep him — he'd never felt more alone.

He wiped his face and walked quietly back to the couch.

SCOTTY CAME RUNNING out twenty minutes later.

"Alex! Alex! Come see what me and Uncle Jaime built!"

Uncle Jaime. Despite everything, Alex almost smiled.

Jaime appeared in the hallway behind Scotty, Jimmy trailing after. One look at Alex and something shifted in Jaime's face. A question he didn't ask.

"Come on," Scotty insisted, tugging Alex's hand. "You gotta see."

Jaime caught Jimmy's eye. Some silent thing passed between them.

"Yeah, come on," Jimmy said, a little too casual. "It's actually pretty cool."

Alex let himself be pulled down the hall.

The Lego set was spread across Scotty's floor — some massive Star Wars thing, half-built. Scotty dropped beside it, pointing at a complicated section.

"See? Uncle Jaime showed me the engine part, but now we're stuck here."

Jaime moved close, shoulder brushing Alex's. "Scotty's too good for me. Maybe big brother Alex can figure out the tricky part. Right, Jimmy?"

Jimmy nodded. "Yeah. Even I couldn't get it."

Alex looked at them. They both knew something had happened.

"Please, Alex?" Scotty whined.

Alex took a breath. "Okay, buddy. Show me."

He sat down beside his little brother, and Scotty launched into an explanation — missing pieces, how the panels connected, what went where. His hands moved constantly.

And slowly, despite everything, Alex felt himself relax. Just a little.

Jaime watched from the doorway, then slipped away.

BILL WAS STILL in the kitchen when Jaime appeared.

Liz was at the stove, not looking at anyone.

"Everything okay?" Jaime asked.

Bill turned. Their eyes met.

"Liz could use some help with dinner," Bill said. "If you don't mind."

He crossed to Jaime, put a hand on his shoulder. Squeezed once.

"Thank you," he said quietly. "For being here."

Then he was gone.

Jaime stood in the doorway. Liz hadn't turned around.

"What can I help with?" he asked.

A long pause. Liz kept her back to him.

"I've got it under control."

"Yes, ma'am." Jaime stayed in the doorway. Didn't leave. Didn't push. Just waited.

Liz wiped her eyes with her apron — absently, like she'd forgotten he was there. But Jaime caught it. He knew.

She composed herself. Straightened her shoulders.

"Well... uh... why... why don't you..." She was searching. "Jaime? Why don't you help with the rolls. Three-fifty. Baking sheet's by the fridge."

She used his name. First time.

"Yes, ma'am."

He found the sheet, arranged the rolls, set the oven. Worked in silence beside her.

Minutes passed. Pots bubbling. The oven clicking.

"You're from New York," Liz said finally.

"Yes, ma'am. Born and raised. My parents have lived in the same apartment since before I was born."

"That's nice." Flat. Polite.

"It is. But honestly?" Jaime glanced toward the window. "I really like the midwest. It's quieter here. Beautiful, too. All that open space."

Liz paused. "I'd suspect most people from New York can't wait to get back."

"I'm not most people, I guess."

They worked in silence for a while. Jaime moved to the celery she'd left on the cutting board.

"Alex talks about you all," he said after a moment. Casual. Like he was just making conversation. "His family. He worries about you. Misses you."

Liz didn't respond. But she didn't walk away either.

"He wants you to be proud of him. I think that's the thing he wants most." Jaime kept his eyes on the cutting board. "My parents are the same way. I get it."

"Mmhmm."

"Most nights we're pretty boring, honestly. Studying at our little corner of the library after dinner. Alex draws while I'm doing problem sets." Jaime smiled to himself. "He's really talented. I don't know if he shows you his work, but it's phenomenal. The things that boy can draw."

Liz glanced over. Just for a second.

"On weekends, if the weather's nice, we'll go hiking around campus. Or Alex will drive us out to see different places — parks, nature preserves. He loves it out here." Jaime shook his head. "It's so different from New York. Quieter. I never knew how much I needed that until I got here."

"Oh really?" Liz said it before she caught herself.

"Yeah. There's this one spot he took me to a few weeks ago — some state park with a waterfall. We just sat there for an hour, not even talking. Just watching the water." He paused. "It was the most peaceful I've felt in a long time."

Liz found herself nodding. She knew that park. Had taken the boys there when they were young.

For a moment, she forgot who she was talking to. Forgot that this was her son's boyfriend. He was just a nice young man helping her make Thanksgiving dinner, talking about hiking and drawing and quiet afternoons at the library.

And then she remembered. And the warmth faded.

The silence stretched. Liz stirred the gravy, not really seeing it.

"You seem like a nice young man," she said finally. Quietly. Like it cost her something to admit.

"I try to be."

Liz shook her head slowly. "It's just... hard. To reconcile what I'm seeing with what I..." She stopped. "You're not what I thought you'd be."

"What did you think I'd be?"

She didn't answer. Couldn't, maybe.

"I don't really know what to say, Mrs. Robertson." Jaime set down the knife. "I just know Alex needs his mom."

Liz turned to look at him. "I don't know what that means anymore."

Jaime didn't have an answer for that. He was eighteen. He didn't have answers for much of anything.

"I don't know either," he admitted. "But maybe you don't have to figure it all out right now?"

Liz was quiet for a long moment.

"I have a difficult time with..." She stopped. Swallowed. "With Alex being..."

Jaime waited.

"...gay."

The word came out cracked. Barely a whisper.

Jaime didn't move. Didn't speak. Just let it sit there.

Liz wiped her eyes. Took a shaky breath. Turned back to the stove.

"The rolls," she said. "Check if they're ready."

"Yes, ma'am."

Epilogue

Two Years Later — Summer

THE STAMFORD APARTMENT was quiet in the morning.

Alex stood at the kitchen window, coffee in hand, watching the city wake up three stories below. Delivery trucks. Dog walkers. A woman in scrubs waiting for the crosswalk. The ordinary rhythm of a New York summer morning.

He'd been here four times now. Thanksgiving last year. Spring break. A long weekend in May. And now this trip — dropped everything to come. Jaime's room had started to feel like his room too.

His little watercolor from eighth grade was there — propped on the small desk by the window, catching the morning light. Alex hadn't thought to bring it. Hadn't even mentioned it when they'd packed. But Jaime had remembered. Had wrapped it carefully and set it here without a word, like it was the most natural thing in the world.

Some things didn't need explaining.

Even Susan had stopped asking if he needed anything and just let him rummage through the fridge like he belonged there.

Because he did. Belong there.

His phone buzzed on the counter. A photo from Jason — him and Brandon at some lake, both sunburned and grinning. *Wish you were here. Tell Jaime we say hi.*

Alex smiled. Funny how things worked out. Jason had been so set on following him to Oakwood — but then Brandon happened, and suddenly Columbus made more sense. They had an apartment now. Jason was at CCAD, finally putting those sketchbooks to use. They were happy. It looked good on them."

Brad had texted last week too — he'd finished his first year at Ohio State, was thinking about studying architecture. *Starting over isn't so bad*, he'd written. *You were right.*

Funny how things worked out. Two years ago, Alex couldn't imagine any of this. Now here he was, watching New York wake up, waiting to meet an uncle he'd spent months tracking down.

"You're up early."

Jaime shuffled into the kitchen, hair still messed from sleep. He wrapped his arms around Alex from behind, chin hooking over his shoulder.

"Couldn't sleep," Alex said.

"Nervous?"

"Yeah."

Jaime's hand found his — the one holding the coffee mug. His thumb brushed across the ring on Alex's finger. They'd picked them out last trip, in a tiny shop in the Village. Alex had said he didn't need the fuss, but Jaime insisted — if they were going to do this, they were doing it right.

"It's going to be okay," Jaime said.

"You don't know that."

"I know you. And he said yes. He wants to meet you."

That was still sinking in. A few emails, exchanged over the

span of a week. And then Chris had written back: *If you're ever in New York, I'd love to meet. No pressure.*

No pressure. Like Alex was going to read that and just wait.

They'd both had summer jobs lined up around Oakwood. Didn't matter. This was too important.

"Come on," Jaime said. "Let's get ready."

THE SUBWAY WAS CROWDED, even mid-morning. Alex and Jaime stood near the doors, swaying with the motion of the train, shoulders pressed together.

"You okay?" Jaime asked.

"I keep thinking about what to say. And then I think maybe I shouldn't plan it. Maybe I should just... see what happens."

"That's probably better."

The train slowed. Their stop.

They climbed the stairs into the summer heat, emerging into Washington Square Park. The fountain was running, kids splashing in the water. Students sprawled on the grass. The arch rose white against the blue sky.

"I've walked through this park a thousand times," Jaime said.

Alex looked at him.

"Wonder if I ever passed them?"

They let that sit. Then Alex took his hand.

"Come on. They're waiting."

THEY'D AGREED to meet by the fountain on the north side.

Alex spotted them before they spotted him.

Two men on a bench. One had gray hair, close-cropped, and a lean face that made Alex's breath catch. Even from a distance, he could see his father in that face — the same jaw, the same way of sitting. But softer somehow. More weathered.

The other man was tall and lean, with dirty blonde hair going

239

gray and an effeminate quality to him. He sat close to Chris, their shoulders touching. Comfortable. Like they'd been sitting that way for decades.

Because they had.

Alex glanced at Jaime. Wondered if all Robertson men were attracted to the same type. Jaime caught his look and smiled — he could read his mind.

Chris looked up. Their eyes met.

Alex didn't pause. Didn't hesitate. He walked straight into his uncle's arms.

The tears came before he could stop them. He didn't know he'd been holding onto this — this grief for someone he'd never known, this ache for the uncle who'd been erased from family history before Alex was even born. It took two years to find him. Two years of searching, wondering, hoping.

And now here he was. Real. Alive. Holding him.

Chris kept pulling back to look at Alex's face, then pulling him into another hug. Like he couldn't believe it either. Like he needed to keep checking.

"You look just like your dad," Chris said, his voice breaking. "God. You look just like him."

Alex felt like a little boy. All those years of missing hugs from an uncle he never knew existed — it was like getting them all at once. Family lore come to life. The ghost story made flesh.

Finally, Chris wiped his eyes. Stepped back. Turned to the man beside him.

"This is Steve," Chris said. Still a little shy with it, even after all these years. "My husband."

Steve didn't wait for a handshake. He stepped in and hugged Alex too — warm, easy, like he'd been waiting for this moment as long as Chris had.

"It's good to finally meet you," Steve said. "Chris has talked about nothing else all week."

Alex pulled back, studying Steve's face. "Wait — are you the one from the rave? In Columbus?"

Steve blinked. Glanced at Chris, then back at Alex. "How did you know about that?"

"My dad told me the whole story." Alex looked between them. "You've been together this whole time?"

Chris and Steve exchanged a look — surprise, and something else underneath.

"Bill told you about us?" Chris asked quietly. "About that night?"

"The rave. The police station." Alex hesitated. "Your father... what he did."

Chris's gaze drifted somewhere past Alex's shoulder. Somewhere far away.

He'd never seen his father again after that night. Never got the chance to hear an apology that was never going to come anyway. And now — thirty years later — here was his nephew. The first family he'd seen since he was a teenager.

"There's a lot he wouldn't know," Chris finally said. His voice was distant. "A lot happened after I left."

Steve's hand found his. Steady. Grounding.

Jaime had been watching quietly. He saw the weight settling over Chris — the old wound reopened — and stepped forward.

"Well," he said gently, "now you've got time to catch up." He held up his hand, showing the ring. "Starting with this."

Chris blinked, pulled back to the present. "Wait — are you two...?"

"Engaged," Alex said. "Next summer."

Steve's face split into a grin. "Congratulations!"

"How old are you two?" Chris was smiling now, the shadow lifting. "God, you're so young."

Old enough," Jaime said with a grin.

Chris reached for Alex's hand, turning it gently to look at the ring. Then at Jaime's. Then back at Alex.

"My nephew's engaged," he said softly. Like he was trying to make it real.

"Does your father know?"

Alex felt his throat tighten. He nodded but couldn't speak.

"It's been a journey," Jaime said gently. "But yes. He knows."

Chris was quiet for a moment. "Still Bill," he murmured. Like he understood something without needing it explained.

"But," Jaime added, "they're coming to the wedding."

Chris stared at him. "They're... really?"

"Both of them," Alex managed. "Dad and Mom."

"I never met her. Your mother." Chris shook his head slowly. "Bill's actually... he's coming?"

"There's a lot Dad — your brother — has been through. With all this." Alex gestured between himself and Jaime. "It took time. But yeah. They're coming."

Chris studied Alex's face. His expression shifted — serious now, protective.

"Are you... you doing okay?" The question carried weight. Like he was remembering his own youth. His own father. Everything that had been done to him.

Alex knew exactly where he was going. "I'm fine. We're fine. Both of us." He reached for Jaime's hand. "Jaime's parents have practically adopted me."

"It's true," Jaime said. "My mom's already planning the rehearsal dinner."

Everyone laughed, and the tension eased.

Chris was quiet, processing. So much had happened. He'd been erased from the family — forgotten, or at least never spoken of. But Chris had never forgotten them. Thirty years of wondering. Thirty years of silence.

"Do..." Chris's voice faltered. He looked down at his hands. "Would you mind if... we attended?"

Alex felt his heart crack open.

Would he mind? He'd assumed — he'd expected — of course they would be there. How could he have not said it?

"Mind?" Alex stepped closer. "Uncle Chris, I wouldn't have it any other way. You're my family."

Those three words.

Chris sat down heavily on the bench, trying to smile but unable to hold back the tears. Steve sat beside him, arm around his shoulders, holding him steady.

Alex looked at Jaime, panicked. *What have I done?*

He knelt down on one knee in front of his uncle. "I'm sorry, I didn't mean to—"

Chris shook his head fiercely. "Don't apologize. You... I've just..." He struggled to get the words out. "I've wanted to hear words like that for..."

He couldn't finish.

Jaime stepped closer, his hand resting on Alex's shoulder. Alex reached out and took Chris's hand.

They stayed like that for a moment. Steve holding Chris on the bench. Alex kneeling before him. Jaime standing behind, steady and present.

"You're my family," Alex said again.

Chris looked up at him. Thirty years of exile. Thirty years of silence. And now this boy — his brother's son — kneeling in front of him in Washington Square Park, saying the words no one had ever said.

You're my family.

About the Author

Michael Manosca first pursued a career in the arts, studying in Chicago, but story-telling has always been at the heart of his creative expression. His travels across the world have shaped his perspective, infusing his writing with the depth and nuance of the people and cultures he has encountered.

Michael writes in a deeply personal format, inspired by the relationships and experiences that shaped his upbringing. He explores the intricacies of friendship, the search for identity, and the quiet moments that define us. Through vivid characters and emotional depth, he hopes to craft stories that linger in readers' minds long after the final page.

When not writing, he can be found wandering the northern woods, exploring new cities, or enjoying a lively conversation in a tucked-away café. He currently resides along the western coast of the United States and is already working on his next story.

Also by Michael Manosca

Beyond Ties that Bind

Treffen

Bloodlines

Prism

Almost Always

Reflections at the Window

Flickering

A Language of Water

Static & Signals

www.ingramcontent.com/pod-product-compliance
Lightning Source LLC
Chambersburg PA
CBHW070729280626
47159CB00023B/2949